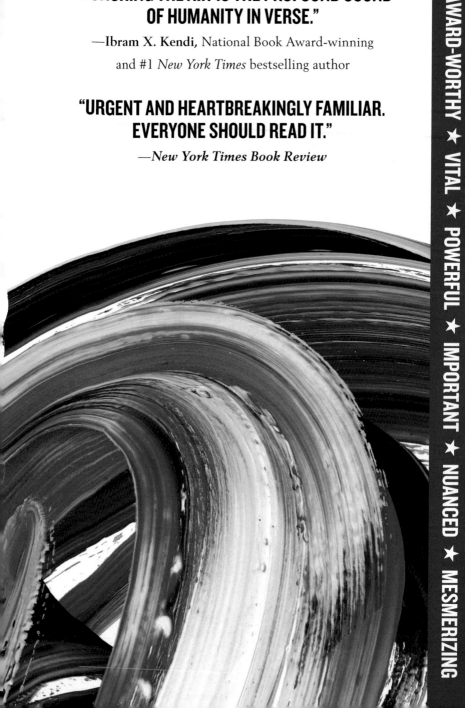

"*PUNCHING THE AIR* IS THE PROFOUND SOUND OF HUMANITY IN VERSE."

—Ibram X. Kendi, National Book Award-winning and #1 *New York Times* bestselling author

"URGENT AND HEARTBREAKINGLY FAMILIAR. EVERYONE SHOULD READ IT."

—*New York Times Book Review*

P9-CJL-164

AWARD-WORTHY ★ VITAL ★ POWERFUL ★ IMPORTANT ★ NUANCED ★ MESMERIZING

PRAISE FOR PUNCHING THE AIR

New York Times Bestseller

USA Today Bestseller

Indie Bestseller

Boston Globe–Horn Book Honor Book for Fiction

Walter Dean Myers Award for Outstanding Children's
Literature Winner

L.A. Times Book Prize in Young Adult Literature Winner

Lee Bennett Hopkins Poetry Honor Award Winner

Time Magazine Top 10 YA and Children's Books of the Year

Forbes Best YA Books of the Year

BuzzFeed Books Best YA Books of the Year

Barnes & Noble's Best Books of the Year

Amazon Best Young Adult Books of the Year

Publishers Weekly Best YA Books of the Year

Shelf Awareness Best Young Adult Books of the Year

School Library Journal Best Young Adult Books of the Year

Kirkus Reviews Best YA Books of the Year

New York Public Library Best Teen Books of the Year

Chicago Public Library Best Teen Fiction Books of the Year

Black Caucus of the American Library Association
Best of the Best Books of the Year

ALA Quick Picks for Reluctant Young Readers
Top Ten Selection

YALSA Best Fiction for Young Adults Selection

CCBC Choices Selection

Top 10 Kids' Indie Next List Pick

Barnes & Noble Children's & YA Book Award Finalist,
Young Adult

Goodreads Best Young Adult Fiction Nominee

"Zoboi and Salaam have created nothing short of a masterwork of humanity, with lyrical arms big enough to cradle the oppressed and metaphoric teeth sharp enough to chomp on the bitter bones of racism. This is more than a story. This is a necessary exploration of anger and a radical reflection of love, which ultimately makes for an honest depiction of what it means to be young and Black in America." —Jason Reynolds, award-winning, bestselling coauthor of *Stamped*

"*Punching the Air* is the profound sound of humanity in verse. About a boy who uses his creative mind to overcome the creativity of racism. About a boy who uses the freedom of art to overcome his incarceration. About you. About me. Utterly indispensable." —Ibram X. Kendi, National Book Award–winning and #1 *New York Times* bestselling author

"In this beautifully rendered book, we are reminded again of how brilliant and precarious our Black Lives are and how art can ultimately heal us." —Jacqueline Woodson, award-winning, bestselling author of *Brown Girl Dreaming*

"A wrenching novel whose story, told in verse, is both urgent and heartbreakingly familiar. Amal's name is the Arabic word for 'hope.' That is what this book ultimately offers, too. Everyone should read it." —*New York Times Book Review*

"*Punching the Air* highlights that wrongful convictions, the school-to-prison pipeline, and the fearmongering of Black bodies are etched in the United States Constitution. It is not easy to break these topics down to adults, never mind children. But *Punching the Air* does so effectively through verse that feels honest and clear." —*USA Today*

"Award-worthy. Soul-stirring. A must-read." —*Kirkus Reviews* **(starred review)**

"This book will be Walter Dean Myers's *Monster* for a new generation of teens. An important, powerful, and beautiful novel that should be an essential purchase for any library." —*SLJ* **(starred review)**

"Prescient and sobering, Zoboi's book is a vital story for young readers in a tumultuous time." —ALA *Booklist* **(starred review)**

"Zoboi and Salaam together craft a powerful indictment of institutional racism and mass incarceration." —*Publishers Weekly* **(starred review)**

"The sympathetic, nuanced portrayal of this young man will have readers holding out hope until the novel's end." —*The Horn Book* **(starred review)**

"A mesmerizing novel-in-verse. The poems—sharp, uninhibited, and full of metaphors and sensory language—quickly establish Amal's voice, laying bare the anger, despair, hope, and talent it holds. Amal's experience of abuse by the system, as well as his peers', incites raw outrage, but his artistic self-expression offers a subtle yet significant kind of hope." —Shelf Awareness **(starred review)**

PUNCHING THE AIR

WRITTEN BY **IBI ZOBOI**
WITH **YUSEF SALAAM**

ILLUSTRATIONS BY OMAR T. PASHA

BALZER + BRAY

An Imprint of HarperCollinsPublishers

For Joseph, and the many lives
you've touched with your art, including mine
—I. Z.

For my mother, Sharonne Salaam, my super shero
—Y. S.

Balzer + Bray is an imprint of HarperCollins Publishers.

Punching the Air
Copyright © 2020 by Ibi Zoboi and Yusef Salaam
Illustrations © 2020 by Omar T. Pasha
(pages 28–29,34–35, 60–61, 64–65, 166, 174–175,
302–303, 326, 356, 366, 367, 380, 381)
Stepback art by wacomka / Shutterstock
All rights reserved. Printed in the United States of America.
No part of this book may be used or reproduced in any manner whatsoever
without written permission except in the case of brief quotations embodied in
critical articles and reviews. For information address HarperCollins Children's
Books, a division of HarperCollins Publishers, 195 Broadway,
New York, NY 10007.
www.epicreads.com

ISBN 978-0-06-299649-7

Typography by Jenna Stempel-Lobell
22 23 24 25 26 LBC 6 5 4 3 2
❖
First trade paperback edition, 2021

PART I

BIRTH

Umi gave birth to me

at home
She has a video
and every birthday
she makes me watch

When I was little
I would run away

Umi would laugh and say
Come here, boy
You gotta remember
where you came from!

She'd chase me around
that small apartment
and I'd cover my eyes and
pretend to be gagging
That's nasty, Mama, I'd say

That's life, Amal
You have to respect it
she'd say

Umi was in this inflatable pool
in the middle of our living room
with the midwife next to her
My father was holding the camera

She was taking deep fire breaths
eyes closed tight, not even screaming
almost praying
Then the midwife plunged
both her hands into the pool

And then
there I was rising out of water
Squirming little brown thing

barely crying
big eyes wide
as if I'd already done this before
as if I'd already been here before

Umi says
I was born with an
old, old soul

OLD SOUL

The thing about being born
with an old soul
is that

an old soul can't tell you
all the things you weren't supposed to do
all the things that went wrong
all the things that will make it right again

The thing about having an old soul
is that
no one can see that it's there
hunched over with wrinkly brown skin
thick gray hair, deep cloudy eyes
that have already seen the past, present, and future
all balled up into a small universe

right here, right now
in this courtroom

COURTROOM

I know the courtroom ain't
the set of a music video, ain't
Coachella or the BET Awards, ain't
MTV, VH1, or the Grammys

But still

there's an audience
of fans, experts, and judges

Eyes watching through filtered screens
seeing every lie, reading every made-up word
    like a black hoodie counts as a mask
    like some shit I do with my fingers
    counts as gang signs
    like a few fights counts as uncontrollable rage
    like failing three classes
    counts as being dumb as fuck
    like everything that I am, that I've ever been
    counts as being

    guilty

CHARACTER WITNESS

We're in the courtroom
to hear the jury's verdict
after only a few hours of
deliberation

and Ms. Rinaldi, my art teacher
was a character witness
It was the first time
she saw me

in a suit and tie
like the one I was supposed to wear

to the art opening at the museum

Or the one I was supposed to wear
to my first solo show in the school's gym

The suit I was supposed to wear
to prom, to my cousin's graduation
to mosque with Umi

is the suit I wear to my first trial

It's as if this event in my life
was something that was
supposed to happen all along

GRAY SUIT

Umi told me to wear a gray suit
because   optics

But that gray didn't make me any less black
My white lawyer didn't make me any less black

And words can paint black-and-white pictures, too

Maybe ideas have their own eyes
separating black from white as if the world
is some old, old TV show

Maybe ideas segregate like in the days of
Dr. King, and no matter how many marches
or Twitter hashtags or Justice for So-and-So

our mind's eyes and our eyes' minds
see the world as they want to
Everything already illustrated
in black and white

ANGER MANAGEMENT

Did you ever see Amal get angry?
the prosecutor asked Ms. Rinaldi

It's the most important question in my trial
        Am I angry   Am I violent   Am I—

Objection, Clyde said

Sustained, the judge said

Did Amal ever display emotions that were—

Yes, Ms. Rinaldi said
That's why I work so hard with Amal
To channel his anger into his art

And I know, I know
that right then and there
she didn't even have to look my way
because she won't see me
She's never seen me
She only sees my paintings and drawings
as if me and what I create
are two different worlds

There's a stone in my throat
and a brick on my chest

WHITE SPACE

In art class
Ms. Rinaldi had said that
the white space on the page

is also part of our illustration
The white space on the page

also tells a story, is part of the big picture
I didn't get what she was saying at first

Then she showed us this painting
An optical illusion, she called it

There was a white face
with eyes, a nose, and a mouth

against a black background
But when I looked sideways

or backward or upside down
there was a black face with

eyes, nose, and a mouth
against a white background

And it was wild how my eyes
played tricks on me like that

but it was my mind that
made sense of it all

It's wild how our minds
can play tricks on us like that

WHITE SPACE II

There were more witnesses
from East Hills
than from my side of the hood
    of the tracks
    of the border
    of that invisible line
we weren't supposed to cross

The couple who just moved in with the baby
who said
We tried so hard to build community

The kindergarten teacher who said
I've always been good to those
neighborhood kids

And the college kid who
recorded the whole thing
and said
I knew something was gonna go down
so I just picked up my phone

To call the police? Clyde asked

Nah, for social, the kid said
It was like a mob
an ambush
So I went live
And no, I've never seen them before

Then when Clyde asked
How long have you been in the neighborhood?

Just the weekend, visiting friends
the college kid said
I didn't think it would blow up like this

That video made you pretty famous, huh?

The college kid laughed
and all I wanted to do was
drag him off that witness stand
But that would've looked bad
Really bad

THE THINKER

I replay everybody's testimonies
in my head
like a song on loop

Their words and what they thought
to be their truth
were like a scalpel

shaping me into
the monster
they want me to be

I'm supposed to be
like a statue
in this courtroom

Chiseled bronze
perfectly frozen in time
like some god
stripped of his power
or a fallen angel
cast into this hell

And every lie
they say about me
        every stone
they throw at me
is supposed to bounce off
like tiny pellets

Here I have to be bulletproof

TWO MOUTHS

What happens if I'm found guilty? I ask Clyde
before the deliberation

He taps his pen on his yellow notepad
as if beating out the rhythm to some rhyme
some party anthem for when   for when
he wins this case

And I want so bad
to grab that pen and notepad
and draw me a victory
a whole scene with dancing shapes
and hard lines turned to joy

That's not going to happen, he says

Umi said English requires two mouths to speak
and four ears to understand

Clyde spoke with two mouths
One for me and one for the court

BLANK PAGE

Mr. Clyde Richter, my defense attorney
is supposed to save my life
is supposed to create reasonable doubt
is supposed to let that judge and jury know
the truth

But he is part of the white space
on my page
where the charcoal and ink
only graze the edges of his world

of Ms. Rinaldi's world
of Jeremy Mathis's world
        the white boy whose entire life
        is a whole blank page of
        this sketchbook
        where this story begins

BLACK INK

So
I am ink
He is paper

I am pencil
He is notebook

I am text
He is screen

I am paint
He is canvas

I am man
He is boy

I am criminal
He is victim

I am alive
He is almost dead

I am black
He is white

FACE PAINTING

Ms. Rinaldi left the courtroom
after the prosecutor showed pictures
of Jeremy Mathis's face after the fight

In school, she said I had talent, a gift
She said my lines were soft
       my subjects were tender
She said I had a lot of beauty
       inside me waiting to bloom

My art teacher of all people should know
I could never make a painting
with the colors of mangled flesh
of broken bone, of bruised skin

out of someone's face

MOVIE STAR

The people who know me
      really know me
are not the ones
the judge and jury want to hear from

It's as if they wanted to hear a story about
some other kid
It's as if they wanted to watch a movie about
some other kid

The prosecutor, with his fancy words
      his hard evidence
wrote the script, directed the scene
      cast just the right actor
to play this kid from the hood
who beat up a white kid really bad
      so bad
      that he can't wake up
      to tell the truth

FAN CLUB

And the truth is
nothing else matters except this moment
right now
when I get to turn around to

look into Umi's eyes
to remind her   to remind me
that she believes me

And I want Grandma to know that
I'm good   I'm good
on the inside

Uncle Rashon knew what went down
even before he saw the news
even before he saw the video
even before he saw the picture of Jeremy Mathis's face

He tried to tell me   He tried to tell me
not to go over to East Hills

My cousins Shay and Dionne tell me
even without saying a word

We got your back, 'Mal   We got your back

The other faces are
from the block   from the hood
from my school   from my past

I don't know if they're watching
this movie with the boy who is playing me
or the real me in this real life

But still, they're here   They're here

My best friend Lucas
       ghosted me
ever since this whole shit went down

BLACK MONA LISA

My umi's face is
           the most beautiful in the world

Skin
like sleeping in on snow days
beneath thick blankets
black

Smile
like an eighty-degree
summer day in April
bright

Eyes
like long subway rides
looking out windows watching
nothing and everything go by in the dark
and letting my thoughts swim
deep

PICASSO FACE

My face must be
      the ugliest in the world

Monster   Predator   Animal
You walk on two legs, not four, Umi said

And since that night
I haven't heard anyone call me boy like she does
          call me little man

Always   man
born full-grown, full-bearded
full of a life not even lived yet
     as if
I've never toddled along the sofa
like in the videos on Umi's phone

I've never eaten mashed-up food and
spit up and babbled with a mouth full of pink gums

I've never cried for a teddy bear or
laughed at Elmo on *Sesame Street*

I've never worn mismatched shoes
and splashed in a puddle

I've never hidden from thunder and fireworks
and angry shouts and gunshots and sirens
                    as if
I've never been afraid of monsters and
predators and animals and

                    my own face

CACOPHONY

The judge takes his seat
on the bench and lets us know
that the jury has reached a verdict

And I can hear everyone behind me
shifting in their seats
whispering
mumbling
crying
as if they know
They already know

Order! the judge shouts
and bangs his gavel

But all I hear is chaos
       All I know is chaos

The disorder of things, places
and people that have no end
no aim, no destiny, no Allah

Godless like hell
Umi tells me to pray, head bowed

submitting to that higher power who
holds the puppet strings

And sometimes I feel like a toy soldier
and I want to beat my chest
to check my bulletproof vest
in this made-up war
like some rap battle
with no mic, no beat, no sound

It's so quiet now
I hold my own hands
My leg is shaking
My heart is a drum
My body—
      I wish I could float into the air
      I wish I could disappear

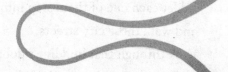

THE LAST JUDGMENT

In the case of the People, the juror says
And I wish I had eyes in the back of my head
so I could see the people behind me
so they can see me

Not the version of me they see in those drawings—
eyes like dead spaces on my face, mouth turned down
nose wide like my father's
cheekbones high like my grandma's

Not the version of me they see on TV—
head down, arms pulled back
wrists cuffed
mean-mugged
name in mud

But the real me, like, past my face, past my story
and into my eyes so they'd know
what really happened that night

I'd let each one of them step into my soul
and walk those city streets
walk through that building's door
walk through that school's halls

sit in those classes
sit on those front stoops
sit on those trains

stand in those lines
stand on those corners
stand in front of this judge

And maybe my whole soul
my whole life
will be like a mirror
And instead of me
here in this courtroom
it would be

the People versus the People

. . . *versus Amal Dawud Shahid*, she says
   Keep my name out your mouth, lady, I say
   But she don't hear me, though
   No one hears me
   My lips are sealed
   but my words have a life of their own

Even if they're locked up
   they'll bounce off three walls and slip between
   metal bars

They'll say *what's up* to the inmates
mean-mug the COs
walk out of the security-tight doors
fly out of this place
aim for the sky, kiss the clouds
and shout to that stale wind
that my name is Amal
and
Amal means hope

The jury finds, she says
As if this is a game of hide-and-seek
and I'm curled up under some table
my body balled up like a fist
     like in my mom's belly
Or in some closet, behind her dresses
smelling like perfume
     like home
     like cooked food
     like plans for the future
     like maybe-somedays
     like see-you-tomorrows

. . . *the defendant,* she says
As if it's my name
As if I came into the world
with fists blocking
boxing gloves like
Holyfield, Louis, Frazier
Tyson, Rocky, and Ali

COUNTING GAME

KNOCKOUT GAME

One count of
attempted murder with a deadly weapon
       The prosecutor had to prove
that I grabbed my skateboard
and swung it at his head
and tried to kill him
But Clyde got that first charge reduced to

aggravated assault and battery with a deadly weapon
       The prosecutor had to prove
that I grabbed my skateboard
and swung it at his head
when his DNA wasn't even on it
so Clyde got it reduced to

one count of
aggravated assault and battery

KNOCKOUT GAME

Shay would punch me on the arm whenever
he spotted a Volkswagen Beetle
That was the rule of the punch buggy game

And I'd punch Shay back really hard because
Umi always said, *Somebody hit you, you hit 'em back*
That was the rule of that game

So I turned down the plea deal
and pleaded not guilty

Because Clyde said it was self-defense

Jeremy Mathis's mother must've
told him the same thing

Somebody hit you, you hit 'em back
Because I threw the first punch

BALL GAME

I really learned about
self-defense
while playing basketball

full court, five-on-five
When the ball
is on their side
and you trying to block
that three-point shot
And they know their turf
better than you do
but you know your
whole team

But still
it's their court
it's their hood

And all you trying to do is
steal the ball, intercept, block
and go home
go home

Go home
is what those people
in East Hills were saying to us

So it wasn't about
who threw the first punch

It was about courts, turf, space
Me and them other boys
were just trying to go home

COUNTING GAME II

On
the
count
of
aggravated
assault and battery—

the jury finds the defendant

        guilty

the juror says

There's a stone in my throat
There's a brick on my chest

The stone turns into a mountain
The brick turns into a building

And it feels like a giant, heavy thing
        like the whole world
is pressing down on me

THE SCREAM

Rage is a deadly feeling, Umi once said   It doesn't move
anything   It just makes you wanna punch a wall or a face It
just sits there, this heavy, dark thing in front of your eyes
making you feel nothing but hunger beating in your empty
belly   So you're forced to face it and open your mouth
wide to swallow it whole, thinking that it will go down
smooth like warm milk   But rage is a thing with
bones and blood and screams that turn into
flames, so you have to chew on it   Take
in all the sharp bitterness that makes your
tongue and mouth and words go numb
You don't even know when it reaches
your throat because it's already there
in your belly   Heavy thing not
moving like a heart stopped

THE SCREAM II

I turn around to see Umi
and the stones fall out of my mouth

But he was still—
I didn't—
Umi—

More stones clog my throat
and I am choking on my words
I am choking on my tears
I am choking
I am
I am choking
I am choking on my tears
and I am choking on my words
More stones clog my throat

Umi—
I didn't—
But he was still—

and the stones fall out of my mouth
I turn around to see Umi

REFRAIN

What was I supposed to say?
That I didn't do it, over and over again
like it's a number-one hit single?
The platinum record of the summer
with a dope beat by some DJ?

That little kids make up dances in viral videos to—
                    I didn't do it
That white girls strum guitars on YouTube to—
                    I didn't do it
That church choirs sing the gospel remix to—
                    I didn't do it
That Ellen does her two-step dance routine to—
                    I didn't do it

And I'm over here
shouting to the judge, jury, cops, reporters
his moms, my moms, that
I threw the first punch but not the last—
                    I didn't do it

BLIND JUSTICE

His mom thinks it's justice for her son

But I know that me and him
both walked down the path
that was already planned for us

And we stepped onto
the tipping scales of Lady Justice
with her eyes blindfolded, peeking through slits
because that rag is so fucking old
worn-out, stretched thin, barely even there

Amal Shahid to the left   Jeremy Mathis to the right
                                             perfectly imbalanced
because where I come from
jail or death
were the two options she handed to us
because where he comes from
the American Dream
was the one option she handed to them

So here we are, blind Lady Justice
I see you, too

THOUGHTS & PRAYERS

There is nothing left to do now
but to think about God

      my country's Money
      my mother's Allah
      my grandmother's Jesus
      my father's American Dream
      my uncle's Foreign Cars
      my teacher's College Education
      my lawyer's Time

When Umi asked for thoughts and prayers
each one of them bowed their heads
to their version of the higher power
and maybe never, ever even once
thinking of Hope

thinking of me

SLAVE SHIP

What happened?
I try to ask Clyde

But the other voices
in the courtroom
drown out my words

And it's like water
is slowly rising
from the floor

reaching my feet
climbing up my legs
as if this courtroom

is a sinking ship
but everybody else
with their freedom

can swim up to the
surface for some air
to safe shores

and I'm the only one
with an anchor
tied to my ankles

Heavy metal
pulling me down
until I drown

So I turn around
to see the freedom
I'm leaving behind
to see the home
I'm leaving behind
I want so bad
to paint this picture
to crop out all the noise
and zoom in on the people
who love me

FAMILY PORTRAIT

Umi's eyes, framed by her blue hijab, are like home
> I know the Quran is on her lap
> with my baby pictures between its pages

Uncle Rashon's furrowed brows are like trips to that
book vendor on the corner
> I know he has conspiracy theories
> about this whole thing

Shay's crooked smile is like when he's losing to me
in a long chess game
> There's fear on his face, like
> this might happen to him, too

Dionne's smirk is like a college brochure
slipped under my door
> There's hope in her eyes, like she really believes
> everything will be okay

Grandma's presence is a whole wide, warm hug
> She's tired, so tired
> I want her to go home and lay down

THE WATCH

The first time I was ever handcuffed
was when I was arrested and charged

with this crime, I thought about
watches and other things I wear on my wrist

In kindergarten Umi got me a waterproof watch
with a Velcro strap, I was always checking it like

I had places to go and people to see and
in second grade I wore those Silly Bandz

on my wrist as if they were status symbols

In fifth grade, the prettiest girl
Tanesha, made me a friendship bracelet

strands of string linked together like chains
That shit never came off, but when we broke up

I tried to snag it loose with my teeth right there
in the schoolyard so everyone could see

that we were done and I'm not about to cry
over no girl, but there go Shawn with his

big mouth talking about, *She dumped you, ha ha!*
So I told him to shut the fuck up right there

in the schoolyard so everyone could see
that I'm not about to cry over no girl

But he kept saying, *She dumped you, she dumped you!*
'Cause Tanesha was the prettiest girl in the fifth grade

and when she was my girl I was the coolest kid in the
fifth grade and you know when you have a girl

all the other girls wanna be your girl, so Shawn
with his big mouth was messing up my game

was trying to make me cry, make me mad, make me fight
and he came to my face one more time with

She dumped your ugly ass! and the only thing left to do
was to deck him in the face, punch after punch

And we were right there in the schoolyard fighting
like we wanted to kill each other but all I was trying to do

was not lose 'cause everybody was right there in the
schoolyard watching, cheering, until   until

the principal came, the gym teacher came
my teachers came to stop us from trying

to kill each other 'cause that's what it looked like
after I was done with Shawn's face

We have a zero-tolerance policy, Mr. Figueroa
said when my mother came up to the school

after I had to sit in the office for a long-ass time
and I knew I was in big trouble 'cause they sent

Shawn to the nurse's office and called his mother
and everything, and I thought I won, I had a rep

for being this hard little kid that nobody could mess with
and I didn't even know how I was supposed to feel—

happy or sad, proud or guilty, like I won or lost—
because Umi's eyes were red when she came to the office

She stared down at me like she was sending lasers
from her eyes, but right behind her was my boy Lucas

51

smiling big and giving me a thumbs-up, but Umi's
face was sad, angry, confused, so I didn't know

what to do with my own eyes when both Ms. Samuel and
Mr. Figueroa called us into the office to say again

that *We have a zero-tolerance policy!* Zero tolerance
What does that even mean? Umi asked

It means that Amal will have to be suspended for
three days and it will have to go on his record

We laid out the rules at the beginning of the school year
No fighting, no bullying, no cursing, no acting out

Zero tolerance
Scholars are learning that our actions always have

consequences and we have to think about
our choices, Ms. Samuel said, sounding like she's a

fucking robot, and Umi was looking at her like she is
and said, *Is the other boy getting suspended?*

And Mr. Figueroa said, *The other boy was sent to*
the nurse's office   He was badly hurt

And then   And then Umi looked over at me
as if I did the worst thing in the world   and

her face   her face looked like it was slowly
slowly turning into   honey falling off a spoon

Sadness moved down from her forehead to her lips
        Drooping and dripping

I'm so disappointed in you, Amal, Umi said
And my   my heart   was like her face

        Drooping and dripping
Then she asked, *Does it have to go on his record?*

Boys fight all the time, right, I mean he's always
fighting with his cousins, kids get hurt   kids

They make stupid mistakes
What's three days' suspension supposed

to teach him?   He'll be home
all alone   I can't take off work to watch him

Umi's eyes were begging for something Mr. Figueroa
wasn't about to give

Ms. Samuel wants us to spread our wings and fly
wants us to reach our full potential

College, it was all about college, so of course
she repeated, *We have a zero-tolerance policy*

and Umi looking at me like I did the worst thing
in the world and Lucas peeking into the office

looking at me like I did the best thing in the world
and Tanesha walking in and looking at me

just looking at me   and me looking at her
and wishing so bad   that I never

got into that fight with Shawn

OCEAN

Ever since that day in the fifth grade when
I got suspended for three days
for fighting

Umi watched me so hard, her rules were so strict
that it felt like I've been trying to
breathe underwater

Every dumb shit I've ever done was me
fighting my way to the top
for some air

CLONE

Ever since that day in the fifth grade

my teachers watched me so hard, so close
that I felt like I was trying to break out of prison
even though it was just school

Every dumb shit I did
they thought it was because of

trouble at home
an absent father
a tired mother
not enough books
not enough vegetables
not enough sleep

They believed those lies about me

and made themselves
a whole other boy
in their minds
and replaced me with him

CONVERSATIONS WITH GOD

Why are you not on their side? I had asked Clyde
I never called him Mr. Richter

I ain't a slave and he's not my Mister
                              Master

Grandma calls me *Master* Amal
because she says
I am the master of my own destiny
I am the master of my own fate
I am the master of my body, mind, and spirit

So there was only room for one master
and Clyde ain't it

(I never tell Grandma that on most days
I don't feel like a master
I don't feel like I'm the one in control)

These things that Grandma tells me
are like
a pan of mac and cheese on Sunday
a pair of socks for my birthday

a whisper in my ear that she'll steal me away
        to take me to her church
a tight hug around my waist and a kiss on my chin
        because I'm way taller than her
These things that Grandma gives me are like
a butterscotch or peppermint candy from her purse

Sweet promises
that make me feel special
only for a little while
Then she goes home
to her church, to her Bible, to her knitting
to her bargain shopping at dollar stores

to her own
sweet
promises

I work for you, Amal
Only you, Clyde had said

So you're in this for the money, I said

Amal— Umi interrupted

He gets to ask me all the questions
and I don't get to ask him none? I said

Then he said, *I'm in it for justice*

And that's when I knew for sure that
my lawyer speaks with two mouths

So when Clyde says, *I'm sorry, Amal*
We did all we could
after the officers handcuff me

I remember that he never really told me
he was on my side

AFRICAN AMERICAN

When I turned thirteen
Grandma told me she'd take me to
    Africa

I told her Africa's not a country
and she slapped my shoulder and
said I'm too smart for my own good

Umi said I should go to connect with my
Muslim brothers and sisters on the continent
and Grandma looked at her sideways

She said her church was organizing
a trip to Senegal and we'd go to someplace
called Goré Island and there'd be something
called the Door of No Return

It's where slaves had to go through
to get on a ship sailing to America
It's where African people lost everything
and stepped out into a future they didn't know

So when the officers hold that door open
leading out of the courtroom

SENEGAL

I think of that trip that never happened
and the Door of No Return

My life, my whole damn life
before that courtroom
before that trial
before that night
was like Africa

And this door leads to a slave ship
And maybe jail   maybe jail
is   is America

COMING TO AMERICA

The officer holding my arm
digs his nails into my skin
squeezing so tight
it feels as if he got hold
of a blood vessel
or something
because my heart   my heart
is suffocating

I clench my jaw and tighten every
muscle in my body

I want to be like steel, like iron
and I'm hoping
that I'm superhuman

THE ENTOMBMENT

The county jail behind the courtroom
is called the tombs
because it's where the system
buries their dead

Clyde told me I won't have a life sentence
and I won't have a death sentence either

I guess this will be somewhere in between
        like Jeremy Mathis

hanging in the middle

Dead to the world
but somewhere in our souls
we are both scratching at the walls
yelling to the sky
punching the air
to let everyone and everything know
that we are in here
still alive

The tombs is where we

wait for space in jail
                        hell
I'm sure   I'm sure

The tombs is where we leave
our bodies so that our souls
can burn in an inferno
I'm sure   I'm sure

This is what Jeremy Mathis's mother
wants to believe
She said it herself
I hope he goes to hell
for what he did to my son

INFERNO

There are other brothers
in here with me
Some my age
some older, some very old

And it's as if all our roads
led to this point
not even crossing
a dead end
with nothing but
concrete walls
and metal bars
boxing us in

We nod at each other
It's our way of saying
I see you, bro
We in here

And that's where the
conversation ends

But we speak with
our hands

our eyes
our bodies

Head back
chin up
eyes wandering
but never landing

We take up space
without stepping over
invisible boundaries

We move around each other
without ever bumping shoulders

Some of us put up more walls
Some of us look as if
                we will break down all the walls
Most of us become the walls

I find a spot to sit
because it feels as if
everything that is alive inside of me
is floating away
I'm not in my body

It's shock, that's all . . . Shock
Grandma had said on the night of my arrest
when I stared out into a void
not here, somewhere over there

I remember that feeling
of being in a dream
or a nightmare
as if this life isn't mine
as if I've stepped into the flesh and bones
of someone else pretending to be me
and I'm waiting for an opening
in the universe to pull me out of
this dream state
this smoky haze
this ghost of a body
that is not me

Sleep is trying to come at me
like a giant ocean wave
pulling me deep   deep

Maybe I can touch the ocean floor
and the ancestors of the Middle Passage
tug at my feet   call me home

Maybe this is the only time
I can breathe
underwater

Shahid!

Who knew that voices
could be so loud
under the ocean

Amal Shahid!
Who even knows my name
under the ocean

And I'm going up for air
floating to the surface
my face staring up

at a sunless, dark concrete sky
Is there an Amal Shahid in here?
Air comes to me in one big gulp

and I almost choke on my own breath
Here . . . here! I'm here!

They laugh at me
And it's the first time

I feel   I feel
          Exposed

They're clownin' me
for being asleep

when the world   the whole world
has peeled back our eyelids
and robbed us of any
                              peaceful rest

Shahid! they call out one more time
You're up next

PROCESSED

It's like I'm meat or wheat
Made into a burger or deli slices
Made into pasta or bread
      Processed
Not the boy I was before the machine
Before the breaking down and pulling apart
Before the adding and taking away

I was made for easy, fast consumption
Like food chains in the hood
      Umi said don't go there
      That you are what you eat

Those jails   that system
has swallowed me whole

RIGHTS

On the night of my arrest
I thought it was the end of my life
It didn't matter that some dude
named Miranda told me my rights
to remain silent   to have an attorney
that anything I say will be used against me

I was silent and Umi got an attorney
I liked Clyde at first because he gave me books to read

To take your mind off things for a little while, he said

BOOKS

The first book
he gave me was
The Autobiography of Malcolm X

And I thought he was
trying to tell me something
because Malcolm was Muslim

Malcolm was a thug
Malcolm was in jail
Malcolm was all about the people

Malcolm went to Mecca
Malcolm said some shit
Malcolm was shot dead

The only book
I gave Clyde was
The Rose That Grew from Concrete

I was definitely
trying to tell him something
because Tupac was a poet

Tupac was a thug
Tupac went to jail
Tupac was all about the people

Tupac went everywhere
Tupac said some shit
Tupac was shot dead

Clyde didn't know
that Umi made me read
all about Malcolm in the eighth grade

Clyde didn't know
that I read about Martin Luther King
and Nelson Mandela, too

Clyde didn't know
that I read big books
and watched documentaries on my own

Clyde didn't know
that I'd reread that book in five days
because after two months

He asked me if I was done

And by that point

I had gotten through twelve books

To take my mind off things for a little while, I said

BOOKED

Getting arrested and being
processed is called *booked*
and that place downtown
is called *Central Bookings*

If Jeremy Mathis
ends up dying
the judge will
throw the book at me

It's as if all the books I've read
will prepare me for all the
books that are coming to me

And Umi worked as a bookkeeper

for small businesses like
Mahmoud's fabric store
Fatima's hair-braiding shop
Mr. Kingston's plumbing services
      and they all came to my trial

Umi didn't have time to read books
There wasn't enough bookkeeping
for bail money, though

MONEY

Bail money is freedom
but it's not free

Bail money means going home
but it's like renting time

Bail money made me feel as if
there was justice

Bail money let me know that
people believed me

Bail money was Umi's friends
and family giving everything they could

Bail money was envelopes
in our mailbox

Bail money became online petitions
and a GoFundMe page

Bail money was
invisible handcuffs

Bail money was a promise
to put back on real handcuffs

Bail money is not going to
save me now

NEW ID

On the day of my conviction
I memorize
>   my inmate number
>   my crime
>   my time

>   On the day of my conviction
>   I forget
>>   my school ID number
>>   my top three colleges
>>   my class schedule

DNA

Before some of us leave
the county jail
the officers chain us—

And I am shackled
again— Maybe these are the
same chains that bind me

to my ancestors—
Maybe these are the same
chains that bind me to

my father and my
father's father and all the
men that came before

him— Linked together
like those DNA strands that
I learned about in

biology— And
maybe I'm not supposed
to break free from them—

This

    is

        the

           first

              time

                  my

              feet

           are

      bound

Where

      the

         fuck

           am

              I

                  supposed

              to

        run

    to

anyway

MIDDLE PASSAGE

There was no
in-between time
to say goodbye

I went from
kid to criminal to felon
to prisoner to inmate

We're moved from
the county jail
and onto a bus
and from the bus
we're going to the
juvenile detention facility
There's not enough of us
on this bus
to fill every seat

So I take one by the window
And it's a relief that my hands
are cuffed in front of me
instead of behind me

I look out and the sky is a slab of concrete
above us
I look for the moon

There are two guards on the bus
one in the front, one in the back
And this almost feels like a field trip
                              almost
Except   Except
the quiet is choking my ears

The absence of voices
is like cold hands wrapping
their icy fingers around sound

And

maybe there was never
this much room on
slave ships

I wanna lay down so bad
I wanna close my eyes so bad
I wanna dream and sleep deep so bad

There's another guy opposite from me
and he looks out his side of the window
just like I'm pretending to be

And if this was another time and place
I imagine the conversation would start like this:

What up, man, I'm Amal— And you?

But he turns to me as if
he felt my eyes on the
back of his head
and says
What the fuck are you looking at?

I go back to my
dark-gray sky

And I feel the heat seconds before
he aims for the back of my head
with his handcuffed fists

It's too late to duck
The blow makes me hit the glass window

It should've shattered
I should've shattered

And I ball up
My head cradled in the crook of my arms

I fold into myself
and I wait for more pain

And that's when I know the story
         that really isn't my story
hasn't made it past the courtroom
yet

The story that I thought
was my life
didn't start on the day
I was born

The story that I thought
was this life
didn't start on the day
I went to that park

The story that I think
will be my life
starts today

Anything that happened
before today

is only the prequel
the backstory

the story behind the story

Nothing before today matters

It doesn't even matter
that I wasn't supposed to be
with Omari that night

It doesn't even matter
that Umi wanted me home by ten
and I knew that she was still out
getting her hair done or something
and she wouldn't even know
          probably wouldn't even care
because I was with Lucas

Except I wasn't

Lucas was with his girl
and I was with Omari
who brought his boy Antwon
who said he had a whole crew
down by the courts waiting for him
for a two-on-two game

and if we came with him
it would be a three-on-three

But I'm not a baller

So I told Omari that I'd rather go
to the skate park
'cause I don't like basketball like that

But he wasn't about to leave his boy
Antwon hanging like that
And I wasn't about to leave my boy
Omari hanging like that

Even though Lucas left me hanging
for some girl
and I wished   I wished so bad
that I had a girl, too
but Zenobia

            Zenobia is her name

doesn't even know
who I am

I bet she does now
Zenobia knows my name

That matters

I tried to tell Omari
that I'm not messing with those
white boys from East Hills
who *been* telling us
they don't want us on their block
like they own that shit
They do   They do

He said, *You with me*
so you good

And I said, *I got my peoples*
waiting for me in the skate park

It was a lie
so he said, *You need to relax 'Mal*
They not gonna fuck with you

And I didn't say
that out here on these streets
on these courts   in these parks
they gotta know you
or know somebody who know you

Out here on these
streets   courts   parks
they will either

speak for you
or
speak against you

And I catch one of these guys
on the bus looking back at me
staring   daring
for me to say something

So this bus   this bus
is the streets   the courts   the park
on wheels   engine roaring
A ship headed for the new world
and we're all in here   in shackles
on our wrists   around our minds
                        around our hearts

So I just let him stare

COMING TO AMERICA II

We're going West
where the sun is
an orange-blue world
a whole colorful star by itself
        falling
                down
                        down
                                down

And under my breath
the words swim
beneath the surface of my thoughts

Under my breath
my rhymes flow like water
And then, and then

They rush to the shore like waves
And then, and then

I overflow
I can't hold it in
I won't hold them in
my rhymes

my words
my truth
are like a tsunami

Will we ever figure this out
Shackling the mind with our consent
Stolen from the natural order of this universe
Shackling the mind with our consent

What do you see when you see me?

The enemy?   The inner me?

How did they trick the untrickable ones?
How did they bewitch the natural mystics?

Yo shut the fuck up! somebody shouts
But I don't give a fuck

I'll tell you   I'll tell you
I'll tell you of a time when I looked back
The lash on my back
The ax on my feet
Making it hard for me to walk a straight line
And with my mouth agape I vibrate
Instead of scream   I can't cry
*   Wishing to die*

My tongue is gone
Last seen on the sand
Near the shores of this land
My eyes lie   My eyes lie
How did they trick the untrickable ones?
How did they bewitch the natural mystics?
I'll tell you
I'll tell you
It was sick

SHUT THE FUCK UP! somebody else says

No! I shout back
    Never
I will not shut the fuck up

HOPE

I hope
that they don't kill me in there

I hope
I can handle the pain

I hope
I have time to heal

I hope
I am stronger than I think

I hope
all the books I've read will save my life

I hope
my brain is a muscle

I hope
I have superpowers

I hope I am superhuman

PART II

AMERICA

We're here
and it's like Allah has closed his
eyes and gone to sleep on me

Night here is dead
Godless almost

But all I see is lights
Not sunlight
or the lights at the end of a tunnel

It's flashing lights on a cop car
It's a flashlight in my face

It's light that makes me want to
curl into myself
like nappy hair in water
getting closer to skin
finding that warm safe place
to hide away from this world

Officer Stanford is what's on his badge
A black dude with a smooth face
who helps the other guys off the bus

I watch how he holds elbows
puts his hand on backs
gentle almost, like a teacher

We're quiet as hell, too
because the only sound that
could come from there

is the hissing of flames
No crying, no yelling, no cursing
just the thick silence of waiting for pain

Stanford meets my eyes
and I look down

It's my turn to step off the bus
and he lends his hand
and I have to be careful not
to step too wide or too far
or else

So I lean on him like he's a handrail
Except   Except

He pulls his hand back real quick
and my step is too wide
the chain is too short

And I see the ground coming
like

a
Mack
truck
at
full
speed

And I swear
I swear
that this time

I
shatter
into
a
million
pieces

I can't hold back the cry
because
I swear   I swear

my face is broken in half

because it's as if I've been
sliced all the way
          down
          the
          middle

Stanford helps me up and
I swear
I left my face on the ground

Wet runs down my lips
and I can't even wipe it off
because maybe what's left
will end up on my cuffed hands

Be careful there, Shahid
he hisses

And I'm still crying like a
fucking baby
because everything hurts

And I feel like punching him
in the face so bad   so bad

But I
only had one fight
before that night with Omari

I didn't always have to throw hands
block fists, dodge punches
before that night with Omari

And I'm ready   so ready
to deck this grown-ass man
right in the face

if my hands   my body   my life
weren't in shackles right now

Let me tell you something, little nigga
he hisses in my ear

And the memory   the memory
comes back to me—

Umi grabbed and twisted my lips
when she heard me say
      nigga
for the first time

I was five
and I thought it was just a word
like any other word
like my ABCs and 123s
like the old heads on the corner
      my cousins from around the way
      my friends at the park
calling me
      little nigga
      little nigga
      little nigga
like it's my name

Don't you ever, ever let me hear you say
that word again, you hear me?
You're not a nigger *and neither are the boys*
you hang around with, nor any boy for that matter
Do you hear me, Amal?

I just never let Umi hear me say it
because at school
on those streets   courts   parks

nigga was like brother
nigga was like homie
nigga was like enemy
nigga was like
      everything that we are, were, will ever be
      ain't nothing but shit
      like Umi had said

Stanford whispers hard like a dull blade
against thick skin

Ain't no movie stars in here
Ain't no fucking celebrities
Ain't no rappers, ballers
none of that shit

Maybe this is what drowning is like
wet (blood & tears)
covering whatever is left of my face

And inside that giant gray building
the juvenile detention facility—
with its bright shining lights
is the bottom of the ocean

I won't be able to breathe down there

AUCTION BLOCK

Shoelaces and belt!
the lady behind the desk in the intake office says
She looks like every other lady back in my hood
but I don't stare too long
because the lights here
the walls here
the glass windows and locks everywhere here
force me to stay alert

And I look down at my wingtips
The ones Umi just bought me

Shoelaces and belt! the lady yells this time

And I unbuckle and pull off the leather
My heart races because these pants
will slip down and I'll have to keep
pulling them up   pulling them up

I always hated it   Sagging

draws showing   ass exposed
I wore mine high, right at the waist
sweatpants cinched at the ankles
with Adidas or Vans

More skater than baller
More blerd than thug
More dreads than fade
More Kendrick Lamar than Blueface
More me than them

None of that will matter here
because I am being stripped naked

I'm dressed exactly like how I imagined
            exactly like how I'd seen in movies
Orange jumpsuit

bootleg sneakers with Velcro straps

And if I squint only a little bit
this place even looks like school, too
with those gray walls and fluorescent lights
It's too clean here
cleaner than my school
and a bunch of other places in my hood

And it smells like nothing
Maybe smelling nothing is like hell

There's even a fading mural of cartoons
Bugs Bunny, Mickey Mouse, a laughing sun
smiling birds and clouds

like this is supposed to be Disney World or something
It's a mix of kindergarten and high school in here

As if bad paintings of smiling birds will
remind us that we're still kids and
the metal doors will remind us
that we're prisoners

and

there are rules
that
force
us
into
straight
lines
like
toy
soldiers
like
robots
like
worker
ants
marching
as
if
we
don't
have
brains

I don't think
I don't dream
I don't write poems
along the cracks in my mind

And I don't spit
rhymes out loud

My face hurts   My body hurts
but I've pushed pain deep down
until it's at the bottom of these
cheap shoes

I walk all over my own feelings
crushing them until
                they are
                      nothing
                            but dust

Shahid, a guard says
when we reach a giant room
with a bunch of blue doors

The doors have slots in the middle
like for hands and food trays
There's also a glass window
big enough for a face to look out or look in

This is your cell
he says, pointing to one of the doors
This is your cell number
Remember it like your life
depends on it

So I try to forget everything
as soon as I step into
this cell
and the metal door slams shut

I want to be a blank canvas now

It's not the blank walls
that make me remember
where I am and what I did

It's not the metal door
or the narrow platform
that extends out from the wall
with its thin mattress
        like padding in sneakers
or the silver toilet that's attached
to a small sink
        like I'm supposed to wash
        my face where I shit
        (And I remember Umi always saying
        don't eat where you shit)
or the row of hooks instead of a closet
        like my new drip
        is ten versions of this orange jumpsuit

It's the loud quiet
It's the voices that I don't recognize
It's the random screams and shouts
It's that buzzing followed by locking metal
over and over and over again
        like each time those doors close
I sink deeper and deeper into hell
I feel it in my stomach now
        the stone that was in my throat
        the brick that was on my chest
The mountain in my throat

the building on my chest
are now an entire country and city
in my stomach

A heavy, crowded, broken place
right there in the middle of me

So I sit on that thin mattress
and hold my head in hand
I listen to my breath
           the only thing I can trust right now
I listen to my heart
And it's the memories that stay with me
           hours after seeing my family
Their faces are still there
behind my eyelids
Their voices speak to me
inside my head
And home calls my name, too
           Amal

I don't forget the sound of the city
cars honking, sirens blaring
the homies on the block talking shit
music blasting

Home has a bass, a rhythm, a groove
so it was always easy
to rhyme to it, to sing to it, to dance to it
to draw to it, to paint to it

Here, there's no music
the silence and the closing of metal doors
and that buzzer like at the end of
a quarter in a basketball game
An alarm telling us that the game is over
again and again   over and over

lights out

GOD, THE ARTIST

Allah is the only artist here
And He prefers the darkest night to be his canvas

He paints the past in broad strokes, bright hues
And the memories dance all over my mind
in living color

He paints in words and voices, rhymes and rhythm
And every whisper, every conversation beats a drum
in my mind
at full blast

He paints in wrong choices, regrets, and broken dreams
And every acquaintance, friend, and enemy laughs at me
in my mind
really, really loud

lights on

WALLFLOWER

The sun is up
It shines through a tiny window
above my narrow bed
The mattress can't even
be called a mattress
There's a small desk and stool
that extends out from the wall
and everything in here is
attached to a fucking wall
and I wonder how long it'll be
before I'm attached to the walls, too

I don't even want to get up
because it's only now
that sleep is finally
pulling at my eyelids

And I wonder I wonder
if Jeremy Mathis has woken up, too

SUNRISE

Someone slips a tray
through the slot in my door

Not food
but close enough
A rolled-up towel, toothpaste
a small bar of soap, a toothbrush
and a pair of black flip-flops

Slow   Slow   Slowly
I do what I'm supposed to do
The things that make me
            still human

The door opens
It's a lady officer
Good morning!
Shower   Breakfast
in the mess hall
Meeting with your officer
and the social worker
Then you start your program
she says

She wears makeup
Glitter eyeshadow
and shiny lips
Her braids are pulled back
like Dionne's   like Zenobia's
She smiles
and something warm rises
in my belly
in that broken place
like sunshine, maybe

PIPELINE

We walk one behind the other
with our hands clasped behind us
Our towels rolled up in our fists

I used to line up like this
in kindergarten
except with a finger on my lips
walking buddy next to me
If I turned around
or spoke or
         stepped out of line
I got in trouble
I always got in trouble
because I always had a friend
in front, in back, and next to me
There was always something
to say   to ask
There was always a joke to tell
to laugh at

But here and now
it's not a classroom, it's a cell block
it's not a restroom, it's open stalls and showers

it's not a lunchroom, it's the mess hall
it's not friends, it's inmates, felons, and delinquents

If I squint
I almost can't tell the difference

CONVERSATIONS WITH GOD II

I know his face
but I don't dare look at it

Stanford sits behind a desk in an office
like he's in charge

The offices here
are like the principal's office
or the nurse's office at school
Places that are supposed to
          help

He motions for me to sit
as he stares at a computer screen
typing stuff about me, I'm sure

Face is looking better
he says

That's not always a good thing here
Don't mess with it
Don't try to heal it
It lets people know not to mess

with you for a while
Somebody already did the job

Still, he doesn't look at me
and I'm starting to not mind
being visible and invisible at the same time

I'm gonna ask you a few questions
Be honest   Don't bullshit me
he says

I got all your basic info
but don't get too deep
I'm not a psychologist
I'm not your doctor
I'm not your daddy
I'm just putting in the data
and someone else will
figure it out

I keep my head up
like Uncle Rashon told me to
I keep my eyes on an empty space
like Uncle Rashon told me to
       even though he never had to
       sit in front of somebody
       who wanted to destroy him

On a scale of one to ten
how happy are you?
Stanford asks

                And I don't have an answer for him
                That question—
                I don't even have words for
                Zero, I say

On a scale of one to ten
how angry are you?

                Eleven, I say

Have you ever tried
to harm yourself?

Have you ever had thoughts
of harming yourself?

Are you having thoughts
of harming yourself now?

On a scale of one to ten
how likely are you to harm yourself now?

                And I wonder if these questions
                are really
                suggestions

CONVERSATIONS WITH GOD III

How are you feeling today, Amal?

> This feels like the principal's office
> except it isn't
> the plaque on her desk says she's the
> SUPERINTENDENT OF JUVENILE
> PROBATION AND DETENTION
> and her name is Cheryl-Ann Buford

> I keep my mouth shut, head down

*Okay, then   I want you to know that you're not
any different from the other boys who come
through my office   Quiet, scared, nervous
I get it and I'm here for you*
she says
White lady with her
hair pulled up, dark-red lipstick, gold earrings

*This is your program   It's like a class schedule
You have the option of taking classes for credit
and receiving your high school diploma or
wasting time, not doing anything to improve your skills
while you're in here   It's your choice*

just like all the other choices you had
but if you abstain from going to class
you have to stay in your cell for the entire day

so I say, *I'll take the classes*

Good, excellent choice, Amal

She gives me a handbook

Read every single word, every single page
Don't worry, you have all the time you need
If you have any questions, let me know
We're here to help you, Amal

I don't believe she can really help me

PIPELINE II

In middle school
I wanted to be a hallway monitor
so bad   but there were rules

You had to have at least an eighty-five average
barely absent from school
perfect uniform every single day
and a mom who brings cookies to PTA meetings

I didn't check off any of those boxes
so me and my boys
clowned all the hallway monitors
even the girls
We threw balled-up paper at them
smacked the backs of their heads
threatened them if they snitched

So when one of them did tell on us
we got suspended for a week
and were assigned our own monitors
for another week because we were on
probation

You have to learn to respect authority
even if that authority is your peer
the principal, Mr. Johnson, said with that deep voice

Umi thought this was a good school
and she tried so hard to get me in—
But I'm thinking it should've been called

      Zero Tolerance Academy
           or
      No Second Chances Charter School
           or
      Prison Prep

SCHOOLED

Ay man, who messed you up like that?

> We're in a classroom, or a room
> that looks like a classroom and
> there are desks like we're at school

Ay, I'm talking to you

> Dude sits right next to me—
> short and skinny with a bad
> haircut—
> and asks this loud enough for
> everybody to hear
> One of the officers who's standing
> by the door
> glances back at us and I know
> this is a test

> *I don't know,* I say

How the fuck you don't know?
It's your face

I swallow hard and look him dead
in the face
and say, *Nobody   Nobody did it*

This class is math
Stuff I learned in the sixth grade
One of the officers puts a
blank notebook
on my desk

The teacher
is a short black man with thick
glasses
I never had a black man math
teacher
ever

Mr. Shahid, is it? he asks
I'm Mr. Bradley   Hopefully
you can catch up   We're
preparing for the GED
or you can work toward
credits for your last school

        I nod   quiet   still   blank

SCHOOLED II

Last summer
Ms. Rinaldi helped me
with my art portfolio to get into
a fancy fine arts summer program

That fine arts program
was supposed to help me
work on my art portfolio
for college

An art college

Why can't I just do a mural
snap a pic and send it to them?
I had asked her

You dream big, Amal
Don't ever stop dreaming big
But for now, put that dream on paper
It's easier to carry around
she said

So I made art on small canvases
She gave me acrylic paints

and drawing pencils that came in wooden boxes
and paper that looked like it was made by hand

I never showed her my poetry, though
I paint with words, too

I got into that summer program

I'm not going to that summer program

SCHOOLED III

Ms. Rinaldi taught AP Art History
and for whatever reason
Advanced Placement seemed to be
only for the white kids at my school

But there I was in my only AP class
          the only black kid in the room
looking at slides of old paintings
and it was boring as fuck
Muted and dull colors
Sad and pale rich white people
doing nothing but looking sad

So I'd pull up my hoodie
and put my head down
There, behind my closed lids
I could paint me a world
that made sense

And there was that one time
Ms. Rinaldi yanked my hoodie
from off my head

If you cannot pay attention in my class
then you don't deserve to be here
she said through clenched teeth

So I picked up my bag
and walked out

I failed the class

She failed me

SCHOOLED IV

No one helped me get into
East Hills High School for the Arts though

Umi bought me
watercolor paint and one big canvas

What if I mess up? I had asked

Let it come the way it comes, Amal
she said

And I drew and painted
painted and drew
that whole summer before eighth grade

The day I had to go in for the interview
I carried my painting under my arm
It was almost my size, my height
and it rained

All those curved and straight lines
all those colors

all those truths
looked like they were crying

I still got into that school, though

SCHOOLED V

Mr. Bradley is trying so hard
to make this like school
Lecturing and solving problems on the board
Asking us questions and expecting answers

But one of the guys—
the one who was asking me all those questions—
starts laughing and cracking jokes

Kadon is his name
and in seconds, two officers come in
and grab him by the arms
and drag him out of that classroom

We get out of the way
when Kadon starts kicking the chairs and tables
and yelling, *Get the fuck off me!*

The other guys laugh
I'm trying not to look shook
And in that moment
I'm glad I have the bruises on my face
It's my mask for now

I wish I had a hoodie to hide under, too
So I slide in my seat
the same way I used to do in
Ms. Rinaldi's class

Invisible

FREE TIME

The dayroom
is the wide-open space
outside the cells
with chairs and tables attached
to the floors
in our cell block

There's a big desk
that sits on a platform
and that's where an officer
watches us
This time it's Stanford

Decks of cards,
cheap, broken crayons
paper, board games
sit in the middle of each table
like this is playtime

They call it free time
and it's the biggest lie
because we are
still in here

BLANK CANVAS

I
have a
crayon and paper
I didn't know that
I could hold this little
bit of freedom in my hands

A blank page   I don't even
know where   to start so I
draw myself   a wide-open
door and then   maybe this is
where I walk   out and into
my freedom   toward free air
Wind blowing   wild like that
day on the   Ferris wheel
when me and   Lucas got stuck
on top and   we just sat
there staring   down at the
world and   people looking
like ants like   we could
just bring our fingers together and grab them one by one
and maybe throw them up in the air We felt like God

And then

somebody grabs the notebook
from right under me
and I'm left holding this weapon
                    this crayon
                    like a weapon

Kadon is back—
and this is how he lets me know that
he's trying to test me

Shahid!
an officer calls out

I don't look up
I don't look around

The officer walks over
His shadow like storm clouds

What are you gonna do with that, buddy?

I look up
It's one of the white officers
who stares down at me
with the sleeves of his shirt rolled up

He leans on the table
His arms close to my face
close enough for me to glance down
at his tattoos

and I stare and stare
and I see what he wants me to see

A black baby
A black baby
with a rope   a rope
around its neck   around its neck

My eyes are glued to that tattoo
I stare
at the details, the lines on the rope
the baby's eyes closed, with tears
coming down its cheeks
Its skin made blacker
against his pale arm

It makes me want to
scream

There's a stone in my throat
There's a brick on my chest

The stone turns into a mountain in my throat
The brick turns into a building on my chest

There's a rumbling in my bones
So I get up and push the table away
wanting that officer to get crushed under its weight
or fly into the air and bang his whole body against a wall
and die   and die   and die

I don't even know when it happens
He grabs me, and in seconds
four officers are on me
pressing my head against the cold, hard floor
a knee is on my throat
my jaw, my face, my head
are being crushed   crushed

This country and city on my chest
splits down the middle
The already broken pieces
shatter and crush
until there is
          nothing
                    but
                         dust

lights out

CUBISM

Umi never made me
lock myself away
stay in my room when
I disappointed her

When the world spins
I shut out the voices
All she would say is
the sun will still rise

no matter how dark
it gets in here
no matter how lonely
I start to feel

I can still be the light
no matter how scared
I get in here
I start to remember

my name is Amal
and Amal means
hope means there
is still a tomorrow

But there's no future in these
four walls   four walls
boxing me in   boxing me in
so I punch the air

shadowbox with God
spar with all four of these
corners as if they are all
different versions of me

Ninety-degree angles
of Amal—sharp lines like
a barber fade, except
I will never fade

I'm still here   still breathing
heart still beating like drums
in some faraway place called
home   home   home   home

CONVERSATIONS WITH GOD IV

Visiting Day goes by last name
in alphabetical order
and happens every other week

S for Shahid
so Clyde and Umi come at the end
of the month
And for a whole week
I counted down
There's enough time here
to keep track of the seconds

There's another big room
outside all the locked doors

It's where the world waits
to meet us for an hour

As soon as I see her
I know Umi is trying so hard
to keep it together
Her eyes are like thick glass
holding in a tsunami of tears
She doesn't cry

She gets up from her seat
and hugs me
I let her hold me
but I don't close my eyes
because maybe I will melt in her arms
and she'll have to carry me home
in her cupped hands

Clyde's voice is like chains
from the other side of the round table
reminding me of where I am
and how I got here

*We can appeal but it will take
a long time, Amal*
Clyde says
*Jeremy Mathis is stable
but he's still under*

and   I wish I had more news

Amal

> *Amal, I'm gonna do everything I can
> to get you out of here
> Everything in my power
> Inshallah*

Umi says from the other side
of the round table

The tables in the visiting room
are some of the few round things
in here
so many squares
so many corners
so many boxes

It's like when white folks
say things like
trying to fit a square peg
into a round hole
this is what they mean
But I'm no square peg

More like a round world
to myself
being forced into
so many boxes

WALLFLOWER II

I'm not attached to the walls yet
but I'm forcing my body to attach itself
to this bed

It's Stanford who comes into my cell
and shouts
Shahid! Come on, let's go!

I hold my breath under the thin covers
Maybe they will think I'm dead and—

Shahid! he yells out one more time
He doesn't come to pull me off
He doesn't come to fight me and destroy me
He closes the door

And I know   I know
that they won't ever force me
out of this cage

CONVERSATIONS WITH GOD V

You can't stay in your room for
days at a time, Amal—
And I suggest you take full
advantage of the hour you have
for Visiting Day—
You're gonna need those memories
of that time with your loved ones
the people who care about you
Cheryl-Ann Buford says

> What I want to say:
> Leave me alone
> Don't talk to me
> Seeing my mother makes me feel like
> > there's a hole in my heart
> Seeing my lawyer makes me feel like
> > he put that hole there

> What I actually say:
> Nothing

THE OPEN WINDOW

Maybe it's been one long day
and somebody else's god
has been switching the lights
on and off
so light and dark
black and white

are like strobe lights in a club
but it's quiet   NO MUSIC
no soul   CLAP CLAP CLAP CLAP

My door is always locked and I watch
through the small window
the guys gathering in the dayroom

taking seats like it's about to be
a meeting or something

and I'm stuck in this box
staring behind the glass

and there's some other dude
in a box banging and telling the guards

to get him the fuck out
They run to his door and

I can't see what they're doing
to him but I hear him cursing

shouting kicking fighting and then
quiet   quiet   and the other guys

are sitting in the dayroom
waiting for something to start and

that's when I see her   gliding
holding something in her arms—

a poster board and markers
She's smiling and the guys sit up

smooth out their sweatshirts
smooth down their eyebrows

smooth out all their wrinkles
their mistakes, their mean mugs

and I think I see them smiling, too
and she looks over at the guards

dragging that other dude
through the dayroom and he's

like a wet sock   subdued
and I wonder for a second if

he's even still alive but that
doesn't matter because she looks

at my door and I make sure
that I'm in that small window so

she can see my face and maybe
she can ask the guards why I'm

stuck in here like that   She can
ask the guards to let me out so

I can see what everybody's
smiling about but she stops

She doesn't smile anymore and she
looks down and she sets up her things

like she's starting the meeting
and I know   I feel as if

she's about to teach something I don't
already know and I know   I feel it

that those guys are not even gonna care
They're just looking at her   just staring

like I am right now   behind the tiny window
in a box   in a box
in a box   in a box

CONVERSATIONS WITH GOD VI

It's only when Cheryl-Ann Buford
comes to my cell
that I at least sit up in bed

Then she says
Is this your way of telling us
that you prefer solitary?
Because we can arrange it

 I prefer *to be in the class that lady*
 was teaching, I mumble

Poetry? Oh, that's a perk, Mr. Shahid
A treat for those who do
what they're supposed to
It's not part of your regular program
You can only participate in
special activities after demonstrating
good behavior, Amal
I'm sorry but you'll have to earn
your way into that poetry class
Cheryl-Ann Buford says

Then she hands me some envelopes
mail from Umi and—

Tell you what, she continues
You can start back with your classes
on Monday and we'll see how it goes
I hope these letters will lift your spirits, Amal
You have to make the best of your time here

What I want to say:
I don't want to do the program
That lady was teaching poetry
and I'd be the only one in there
who would even care and
who would listen
to every word she says
every word

What I actually say:
Nothing

My dear Amal—
The only way to survive hell
is to walk through

Amal—
You have to meditate
study your Quran
do your daily prayers
ask for forgiveness
courage and strength

Amal—

Umi's letters are too soft for this place
They force me into a bubble
make me float into thick air
and then with just one shout
one slamming of a metal door
one guard yelling my name
or my inmate number
I will burst

The first time I feel something
other than stones and bricks
on my chest

is when I see the name
on one of the envelopes
I read it over and over again
to make sure that
the arrangement of letters
the handwriting
the words
are what I think they say
are who I think it is

Zenobia
Zenobia
Zenobia

Part of me wants to
wait to open it
Part of me wants to
tear it open
So I place it under the mattress
like cash
and save it for when the day comes
when I can't take it no more
and I feel like my heart is
about to split open

This letter from Zenobia
will be here waiting for me

like glue
like Grandma's needle and thread
to fix me and put me back together again

But   but
what if she's waiting for me
Time is different for her

So I open it slow   slow
slowly
and—

Dear Amal,

I'm not into writing letters and all. People don't even write letters anymore, but anyway. I hope you don't mind my handwriting. You probably don't remember me. I know you have a lot on your mind and some girl from your school is the last thing you'll be thinking about. You probably don't even know I exist. At least that's what I thought, until Lucas told me the other day that you've been checking for me since freshman year. I don't know if it's true or not, but why would he say that if it wasn't?

I guess you want to know why this random girl is writing you. Amal, I'm so sorry for everything that happened to you. And in case anything happens to you in there, I wanted to let you know that I believed you the whole time. I'm here if you want to write back.

Zenobia Angel Garrett
(The girl with the blue braids)

THE BRIDGE IN THE RAIN

Now she tells me this?
When I can't even see her?
When I can't even talk to her?

If I cry
right here
in my cell

with no one
to see me

It'll be like
a rainstorm
over that broken
country and city
on my chest

It'll be like
a hurricane
leveling a whole
city and country
and I would have
to build new ones
on my chest

MICROPHONE

Instead I bang out a rhythm
make the door a drum

make my fist a mic
make my words a bullhorn
make my truth the air

Stop killing, brother
you are already marked
because of your color
So why not put us all in jail?
Chance we'll become like snails
Chance we won't rebel
On me, they left indelible scars
I'm over here spitting rhymes behind bars
They thought the box would get me
like Kunta in captivity
but I'm still free

Up north I come from down south
with the greatest tool
my mouth my words my rhymes
dark in skin tone like the dapperest of Dan

talking about history
too many young folks
living in mystery

things I have read
and talked about
all this bloodshed
all this death
but neither hurt my ears
nor left my eyes in tears

I overcame fears
not afraid to take a chance
'cause pain grips my heart
as I look to the motherland
I am here in captivity

Who is more free
                    you or me?

HYPE MAN

Somebody claps from the empty dayroom
and his face shows up in the window on my door

Kadon   So I step up to face him
and he smiles   white teeth showing   eyes bright

A test   So I keep a straight face, straight back
there's only this metal door between us

but I'll be on the other side of that door soon
and he'll be waiting for me
and I'll be waiting for
pain

but

Yo that shit was fire, he says
still smiling   eyes still bright

*When they let you out your cell
we gonna connect,* he says

                        And we do

in the mess hall

they let me out for lunch
but I have to see Ms. Buford again

and Kadon comes over
with his tray as if this is high school

He holds out his fist for a pound
I take it   to show him respect

even though I don't know
what this is all about because
this ain't high school

And he makes the table a drum
He makes the air a mic
He makes his words the air

Material things
selling drugs for
blue or red colors
Flipping has me turning
against my own brother

The unwise are at the mercy
of the wise
They did not realize
until a family member died

Now tell me why
you want to be in the belly of the beast?
A dumb man sings a dumb man song
The devil's advocate is trying
to make you his feast

Somebody says
Yo shut the fuck up, man!
Ain't nobody wanna hear that shit!

Two guys walk up to us
An army starts to form
behind them
And I know this scene

This is when I'd leave
the skate park
The wheels
under my skateboard
like wings

This is when
I didn't leave
East Hills
that night with Omari

And this is when
I can't skate away
I can't walk away
I'm stuck here
like that night
with Omari

Kadon shuts up
lowers his head
and turns away

I do the same
I'm not stupid
but—

Ain't you that kid?
one of them asks

                    Yeah, I say
                    turning
                    and looking him dead in the eye

He nods
chin up, eyes down
like
I see you
Almost like respect, I think
I'm not sure
But the guys behind him
won't stop staring
and—
I'm like Kadon again

Head down
back turned
Defeated

When those guys leave us alone
it's like dark clouds parting
Still, there's no sun
Just a little bit of light
for me to see Kadon's face
  Black eye
  Swollen and busted lips
  Eyes moving way too fast
  He keeps cracking his knuckles

We heard you was coming, he says
They don't let us watch the news
but we still get the news in here
But be careful, though
They're watching you

CONVERSATIONS WITH GOD VII

Cheryl-Ann Buford asks
Are you ready to start your
program again?
I see you made a new alliance?

   Kadon? I ask

Yes, Kadon
and all that rapping
you two are doing—
Being here isn't the set
for your music video, Amal
she says, leaning over her desk

   What I want to say:
   So you're telling me to shut the fuck up
   just like everyone else

Listen, Amal—
You're not going to get a record deal
out of this—
What you do and say here will not
be part of your mixtape—
This is serious and this is your life—

Your life, Amal—
Do you understand me, young man?

MEDITATION

I had folded a piece of blank paper
and slid it behind the elastic waist of my pants
I took two pencils with me into my cell

And I have a few minutes before it's lights-out
so I start with her name   Zenobia

The words don't come
I doodle along the corners
curlicues and flowers and pretty shapes
and I start with a letter   I

But the words still don't come
So I write out her name
over and over and over again
Z

       Zen

              Zenobia

And then
the letters in her name
become
light and dark lines
that become the

curved lines of a pretty face
that become
       Zenobia

This is what I send her
to let her know that
I saw her
I see her
I remember her

Zenith, you are the highest point in the sky
    where one day I hope we will meet again

Everything about you is from heaven, angel

Nothing about you is from this earth, this planet
    you are from a whole other world

Optimistic, you give me hope for the next day
    and for when I can see your smile again

Beautiful, I can draw you a million different ways
    and the lines and curves of your face will always be
    shaped into a masterpiece

Intelligent black girl, book smart with a bright future

Always keep me in your heart, Zenobia, even if time
    moves you away from me— I will always remember
    you remembering me

lights out

GUERNICA

Today is Friday

I'm standing in line
waiting for a shower
Soap in one hand
towel in the other

I've learned to be fast
the same way Umi taught me
to do on cold, busy mornings
before school
but like I said
this ain't high school

So when I'm pulled out of the line

by two of the guys
who had stepped to me and Kadon

I drop my soap and towel
make my body an earthquake
but they are mountains
and they drag me to some dark room
and close the door

I take
blow after blow
after blow after blow
until my breath is a dragon
hot flames
ignite in my soul

The taste of copper
rises out of my belly
and pools in my mouth
I know better than to wipe it off
I know better than to cry

And they leave
my body limp and heavy
The cold floor
against my skin
is an ice pack

What if hell is a frozen place
I'm there   I'm there
and I might die here

DUST

They can't kill you in here
but they will try, Umi says
from across the round table

That's the point
Locking you up isn't enough
for them   They will try
to crush your spirit until
you're nothing but—

                    Dust
                    we both say together

And what does dust do, Amal?
What did Maya Angelou say about dust?
Umi asks

                    It rises, I whisper

You gotta say it loud enough
for me to hear it, baby—
Loud enough for you to believe it

Dust rises, I say
loud enough for it to
ring in my own ears

She takes both my hands
and squeezes them
but I pull away from her

Don't call me baby
not here, not now
I say, loud enough for her to hear

Those guys didn't touch my face
so she doesn't know how my
insides have already
turned to dust
and it can't rise
because it's trapped here
in my belly

Amal—
No matter how tall you grow
No matter how thick your beard
No matter how deep the bass in your voice

You were first my baby boy
grown into a young man

growing into a man
becoming an elder
transitioning into an ancestor
evolving into spirit
turning into breath
easing into life

You are my life
and you are life itself
Amal—

What I don't say:
Umi, you gave me life
You
And these words are stuck
in my throat like stone
Everything I don't say to Umi
becomes a mountain
becomes a country of
unspoken things

What I actually say:
You don't have to come
here so often, Umi
I know it's hard
I know it's a long trip

How dare you say such a thing, Amal?
You are not alone in this fight
I'm here with you, always
Your struggle is my struggle
Your hurt is my hurt
I'm hurting because you're hurting, Amal—

FAMILY PORTRAIT II

I look up and around
at all the other guys
with their people

Their mothers   their sisters
their brothers   their uncles
and maybe, maybe their fathers
with their smiles, frowns, worries
fears, joys, pains, heartbreaks
written all over their faces like poetry

Their bodies—
how they lean across the tables
holding hands
how they cross their arms
protecting everything
how they pull out stuff
from bags like it's Christmas—
If only they could be still for long enough

I would paint this whole scene
for the world to see

And Kadon, my hype man
is with an older and taller version of him
Same eyes, same small nerdy frame

and I wonder   I wonder
how he ended up in here
with a pops like that

So I ask Umi
Where's Uncle Rashon?

And she says
It's gonna take him a little while
This   This really hurt him
He wants to see you, Amal
He really does

EXPRESSIONISM

Those white boys are gonna
body you in here, Kadon says

Or they'll die trying

                       They know about East Hills?
                       I ask

He looks at me like
I just asked the dumbest question

                       We're in the mess hall for
                       breakfast and word got around
                       that they got me, they got me
                       for Jeremy Mathis
                       They got me for all the things
                       they heard about me
                       all the things
                       they think they know
                       but I can't say that I didn't do
                       what they think I did

                       They can try, I say
                       keeping my head down

                    eyes up, looking around
                    but never at or through anyone
                    just around   aware   alert

at how they all put themselves
into groups, squads, teams, gangs

Back at East Hills High School for the Arts
we were like a paint palette

blending into each other
in swirls of color, shade, hair

size, height, values, souls
memories, intelligence, beliefs

Here, we're not even paint
We're a box of cheap markers

that don't even blend well
The shit that forces you

to stay in the lines or else
the colors will bleed

The colors will bleed

CONVERSATIONS WITH GOD VIII

She's not God, really
But she acts like it
and they put her in charge
of us here
She asks questions
says stuff
and she writes down
what we do and say into her little computer
And all that gets sent to the real God here
  The judge

   So I sit up in the chair
   across from Cheryl-Ann Buford
   and say

   I write poetry and I paint, too
   That's all I wanna do
   I just wanna do my time and—
   I don't know if y'all give a fuck about
   that, but—if I write and draw and paint
   maybe I'll get out of here alive
   My voice cracks and my throat is dry

She looks at me as if I have two heads
and says
What on earth makes you think that
you won't get out of here alive, Amal?
Think about the fact that we offer
a creative writing class
And yes, if you want to paint or draw
you can do that, too
But there are rules, young man
With all the officers we've got around here
do you think we need more?

       No, I say, swallowing hard

She leans over her table
like I'm about to snitch

Did something happen to you
to make you feel unsafe, Amal?
Because if something did happen
to you, we'll have to report it

       No, I say really fast
       Nothing happened

WHITE SPACE III

I felt safe
at East Hills High School for the Arts

Nobody was trying to mess
with some art kids
carrying around portfolios

Kids with piercings and tats
boys wearing nail polish
and girls wearing bow ties

Black kids who listen to metal
and white kids who listen to trap

We were weird and free—
a bubble in the world
that would burst open
at the end of the school
when we all walked out of its doors

But still

Ms. Rinaldi gave me hell
because I didn't fit

into her definition of weird
I was a different kind of weird

> my hair too wild
> my skin too dark
> my voice too deep
> my paintings too colorful
> my art too free

Amal is disruptive
she wrote on my report card
Amal needs to focus
Amal is not prepared for an
> *advanced-level class*

She failed me
over and over again
until—
She thought she could
save me

lights out

THE PERSISTENCE OF MEMORY

In my cell at night
the worst thoughts swim around

my mind when I'm locked up
in a box with nothing but the
quiet darkness as my hype man
my producer, my DJ
and just the memory of making music
the memory of hearing some new joint
for the first time

So I try to make my own
Pull a rhythm, a bass, a beat
from out of the stillness
and I wonder   I wonder

If I'll die right this second
or tomorrow or the next day

Umi doesn't know that they
can kill me in here
and say I deserved it

They will make me pay for
what I did to Jeremy Mathis

Promising college student
they called him
as if the life he was expected to live
wasn't a guarantee

Quiet kid with no problems
they said
as if his yearbook picture painted
his whole life story

They don't know   they don't know
that it all started with him

starting with me

                    Starting with the moment
              I decided to go with Omari to the courts

          There were some guys I've never seen before
              and when I spotted them I knew

              that they were from the other side
          of the park—not where the projects are

not where people know me and know my name
and Umi's name and know my face and my voice

They were from where the big houses are—
McMansions we call them—and those houses

were filling up with new faces   Those white boys
were from where Mr. George and the Kingstons

got their houses sold and bought from right under them
I've heard the word before—gentrification

But we lived in the same building I was born in
and paid the same rent my whole life, so we were good

But on the other side, the big houses
(some painted in bright colors, others run-down)

got fixed up nice and painted over in grays and beiges
making that part of our hood look like a futuristic suburb

and soon there was this invisible line we couldn't cross
like we can't go where the nice places are

Can't touch the nice things because everything about us
our skin, our faces, our hair, our words, our music

                                    will break things
                                    will ruin things
                                    will make things ugly

                                    just by us being there

But those white boys
didn't care about no lines

The world belonged to them
including our hood

So when we saw them
using the courts as their own

little skate park, of course
we were like *get the fuck out!*

Not me, but Omari and his boys
because I was too busy

checking out their tricks
their ollies, their kickflips,

their heelflips, their no complies
and this one dude skated

right past us with his
middle finger up and I

laughed but Omari and his boys
didn't   They got heated

and said
all kinds of shit to that dude

and that second I knew I had
to make a move because
I thought of Grandma and
her prayer for me   her promises for me

That I am a master
of my own destiny

        The worst thoughts swim around
        your mind when you're locked up
          in a box with nothing but the
        quiet darkness as your hype man

      and I was definitely Omari's hype man
      that dark night but it was far from quiet

        I've never been to a club, really
          never been to a good party

where the music is so dope
that you feel it in your bones

I've never been anywhere that
made me feel like I was losing control

of my body, my mind, my actions
until that night

There were five of us

Four took a plea deal
and were sent straight
to a juvenile detention facility

I went to trial and was found guilty
and I'm sent straight
to a juvenile detention facility

BLIND JUSTICE II

All because

we were in the wrong place
we were in the wrong skins
we were in the wrong time
we were in the wrong bodies
we were in the wrong country
we were in the wrong
were in the wrong
in the wrong
the wrong
wrong

All because

they were in the right place
they were in the right skins
they were in the right time
they were in the right bodies
they were in the right country
they were in the right
were in the right
in the right
the right
right

We were
a mob
a gang
ghetto
a pack of wolves
animals
thugs
hoodlums
men

They were
kids
having fun
home
loved
supported
protected
full of potential
boys

lights on

wake up
fix bed
brush teeth
shower
breakfast

PROGRAM
Math
English
LUNCH
Free Time/Recreation

Poetry?

SCHOOLED VI

Being in classes here
feels like being in regular school
And it's wild how I can't even
tell the difference
except we're all wearing the same
orange jumpsuit
But we still have to learn shit
that keeps even our minds in cages

That's what Uncle Rashon always says
That school teaches you *what* to think
not *how* to think and nobody raises
their hands except to give
the right answer
The teacher only
asks questions to hear
the right answer

So I do
the same way I used to do
in Ms. Rinaldi's class
I ask questions
If we're convicted felons
what's the sense of learning this

if we won't be able to get a job
when we're out?

The other guys shift in their seats
and mumble under their breath
the same way the kids in art history class
used to do

PIPELINE III

I remember that time
when we had a final
and Ms. Rinaldi
was showing slides of old paintings
we learned about

We had to memorize
the artist's name and the year
      it was painted
Extra credit for naming the style and country
like Michelangelo and the Renaissance in Italy
Monet and Impressionism in France
Picasso and Cubism in Spain

Halfway through the slides
I raised my hand and asked
Did other people around the world paint
or just old white men from Europe?

Everybody laughed
She sent me out of her class
and failed me for being disruptive
I was supposed to go to the principal again
But I just walked out of the building

and didn't come back for a week
        I suspended myself

But then the school called Umi
and she was tired   so tired

of yelling at me
of trying to get me to focus
of trying to get me to try

Umi said
I had big dreams
I had huge talent

but I fucked up my grades
in school or maybe
school fucked up
my life   It's hard to tell

But I'm sure about one thing
I'm not dumb
I know my math, my science
my English   all that shit

I especially know my
art and words

How to bend and twist
them into
truth

I know
it's hard to tell
just by looking at me

BROTHERHOOD

We have assigned seats
in the classrooms, but
Kadon still ends up next
to me as if he's watching me

During free time in the dayroom
he drops a deck of cards
on the square table
where I finally   finally
have a notebook to myself

and I'm careful not to write
not to draw anything yet
So I sit there staring at the
blank pages

Ay man, you gotta make sure
you keep up with the work
Once you get outta here, you'll
have all or most of your credits
Kadon says, while shuffling the deck

        Amal—my name's Amal
        I say

Nigga I know what your name is

        I'm not a nigga

Oh you one of them *niggas*

Some other guy comes to sit next
to Kadon, and then another, and
another, and soon I'm surrounded

        At least these aren't the
        white boys who beat up on me
        but still

What, you think you the shit
just 'cause you been on TV?
one of the guys says

This is juvie but that dude
looks like a whole-ass adult
so I don't look him in the eye
I don't look up from my blank
notebook at all

You a high-class criminal?
You a bougie gangsta?

I'm neither, I say

I'm neither, he repeats
That white boy was your homie
Y'all got into a lovers' quarrel
or some shit   He end up half dead

I don't even think about it
but I raise my hand to put
pencil to paper
finally   finally   I'm drawing
I start with a curved line
some shading
eyes, nose, mouth   mangled
all this to keep me from
spilling words
that will make me want to swallow
them back   Say things that I'll

regret
So I draw and draw

And he pulls the notebook from
right under me

        Before I can even throw a punch
        Kadon and some other guy hold
        me back   even while
        I turn into a storm   Rage
        brewing in the pit of my belly

You really need to calm the fuck down
I was talking to you and you should've
been listening—
What I was trying to say is

You one of us now
You one of us

BROTHERHOOD II

I'm
not trying
to be part of no
gang or crew, that's the
shit that got me in this mess
in the first place, I tell Kadon dead-ass
knowing that here, I don't have a choice

CUBISM II

Kadon says I need them
Kadon says they got my back
Kadon calls them homies

I call them
more corners

boxing me in   boxing me in
boxing me in   boxing me in

ART SCHOOL

Today is Friday

and I did everything right this week
I followed the program
like I'm a robot, no brain
except when I had to pretend to use
it in class, dumb shit I already learned

Filling out worksheets and taking practice tests
but in my notebook, I drew myself another world
another opening to other places, other dimensions
and Kadon was right
I needed a crew to sit next to me
to be my four corners so that I'm not cornered

There's Amir with the locs down his back
Quiet like air, like there's a heavy secret
behind that silence

There's Smoke who wears that name
like a bulletproof vest   I swear
he can see through people

There's Rahmarley with the braids
that stick up like antennas and
he thinks he could read people's minds

and Kadon

I get it now
those white boys don't see me
and I don't see them

But I get to see her, though
finally

And she comes into the dayroom
gliding   holding something
in her arms—a poster board and markers

I see her   smiling
                and I sit up in my seat
                smooth out my sweatshirt
                smooth down my eyebrows
                smooth out all my wrinkles
                my mistakes, my mean mug

I'm happy to see you here
she says

even though she doesn't look happy
Her face is serious, like
she means business
even though she's teaching poetry
My name is Imani Dawson
and I'm a poet, educator
and activist—
I like to call myself
a prison abolitionist

> *Prison abolitionist?*
> *I ask*
> *Like in slavery?*
> *So you're here to free us?*
> *Okay, then   So my name is*
> *Amal   and*
> *I don't like to call myself a slave*
> *but here we fucking are—*

And they laugh at me

Unacceptable, Imani says
Let's try this again
By calling myself a
prison abolitionist
I mean that I'm part of
a movement

that is fighting to abolish
the prison industrial complex
as we know it
And no, Amal
you are not a slave
None of you are
I'm here to help you
remember that

                Amal, inmate
                is all I say

Who are you, Amal?
What is your truth?
she asks

                I look around, no one has their
                eyes on me   so I shrug

Everybody was
stumped by that question
when I first asked it to the group
It's okay, Amal
You have time to think about it

What is your truth?

She turns away
and writes on her poster board
with a blue marker

MISTAKES & MISGIVINGS

Take a sheet of paper out
of your notebook and
fold it in half, she says
without looking back at us
On one side you write
"Mistakes," on the other side
you write "Misgivings"

> My page is still blank
> I don't do what she says
> This shit is for kindergarten
> Too many questions
> too many directions

Where's your work? she asks

> *I thought we were just gonna write,* I say

You are *writing, you have to start*
somewhere, Amal

I'm not trying to make
origami   I just wanna write

Oh, *so you're a* serious *writer*

Not like essays or stories, but
just the truth

Truth— Well, let me see what you got
Follow the directions and take it
one word at a time— One word at
a time, Amal—
Mistakes and Misgivings

What I want to say:
What does that even mean?
Why can't we just write?
Why does everything have to have
rules   directions   order?
We're already trapped in boxes
why can't we just be free with this?

What I do:
Crumple the paper and walk
out of the dayroom and toward
my door

The officer with the tattoo—
his name is Beale, but I call him
Tattoo
so that I remember—
tells me to get back
to the dayroom, but I don't move

Where the fuck do you think you're going?
he hisses

I stand there in front of my door
waiting for him to pull out the keys
He holds his arm in front of me
and I see that tattoo again
that tattoo again

You go in there, you'll stay in there
Forty-eight hours minimum
he says, opening the door

and I walk in

THE ENTOMBMENT II

The metal door slamming shut
behind me
makes my insides sink
to the bottom of my feet
to the bottom of these
cheap sneakers
to the cold concrete floor
to the basement of this place
to the soil, to the bedrock
to the middle of the earth
and I bury myself
way more than six feet deep

This cell is a tomb

I left my notebook up there
I left my pencil up there

Down here in the dungeon
of my mind

I write anyway
I draw anyway

The pen and pencil
are my thoughts and memories

The paper is my soul

and Imani's voice echoes and
bounces off the bedrock
lingers in the heat
repeating   repeating

MISTAKES & MISGIVINGS
MISTAKES & MISGIVINGS
MISTAKES & MISGIVINGS

I learned about this thing
called the butterfly effect—
not in school!
but from the guys on the block

It was this one dude
who said that's why we're always
fucking up, we're always making mistakes
because ain't no butterflies in the hood

See, if there were butterflies
we would have what's called
the butterfly effect

A butterfly's wings can
change the path of a storm

Something so small
can change
one big thing in the world
one big thing in the universe

If there are no butterflies here
no pretty little wings flapping in the hood
then we can't change a thing, he said

It's a metaphor, I said

Ain't nobody ask you, he said

We're the butterflies, I said
and the things we do are like wings

We do shit every day, he said
How come shit ain't changed

Nah, I said
Everything is changing something
every day, even this conversation

I draw a vertical line on the wall with my finger
I can't see it, but it's there

To the left I outline the word
MISTAKE

To the right I outline the word
MISGIVINGS

MISTAKES

I should've stayed with Omari
that night
I should've just went home
that night
I should've just went on the PS4
that night
Umi should've been home
that night
I should've never met Omari
that day
I should've shooted my shot with Zenobia
that day
I should've went with Lucas
that day
I should've just walked away
that second

MISGIVINGS

Something wasn't right about those
guys on the basketball courts
I felt it in my gut

So I turned back and left
Omari with his boys
to deal with it

Something wasn't right about
that night, the way
the air felt

around my body as if it was
trying to warn me, trying
to keep me away

but I skated all the way
to the other park
where I knew

it was safe, where people
knew my name
and my face

But by the time I got there
they were leaving and
skating out of

that park and onto the streets
like we usually do
We were home

We knew the twists and turns
of every block in our hood
We knew the faces

the music, the grandmothers
calling out of windows
We knew the kids

and we knew the lines
but that night the air
was just right

and just wrong at the same time
One of them said there's this
hill over on the other side

There's these steps with a handrail
where we could skate and where we
knew there was a line

and we didn't even know that
they were following us
No, chasing us

out of that part of town where the
hood stopped being the hood
and became a town

They came on bikes and skateboards
and we didn't run, we stopped
I stopped and waited

This time, this time
I stayed and it
wasn't even

for anybody
for no friend
for no homie

I stayed to defend myself
even though everything
about that night
that moment
was telling
me what

they
told
us
GET THE FUCK OUT

In my cell
I crack
I break
I split in half
down the middle
I shatter into pieces

and BANG and BANG and BANG and BANG and
BANG and BANG and BANG and BANG

on that door   on those four walls   at those four corners
yelling
shouting
screaming
clawing
to

GET THE FUCK OUT
THE   FUCK
FUCK   THE
OUT FUCK THE GET

PART III

HOPE II

Maybe   Maybe
she wrote me back
or drew me her world

When we get letters from the outside
we line up and collect the envelopes
like it's payday

We can't buy anything with these words
Empty, sweet promises from people
whose love was not enough to keep us free

I don't open the ones from Umi
I don't open the ones from Grandma
but seeing her name again sends a wave
over me like hearing new music
for the first time

I hold the one from Zenobia
close to my chest
and save it for later
It'll be there waiting for me
for when I need a cool drink of water
after another war

I can't believe she wrote me back

HOPE III

Jeremy Mathis is showing
signs that he might
wake up soon
Clyde says from across
the round table
He'll have to make a statement
and hopefully he'll remember
what happened that night
But you have to follow the rules
and do what you're told
Follow your program
get your class credits
and before you know it
time will go by fast
and this will all be behind you

If he wakes up and tells the truth
and you've been on good behavior
There's hope, Amal—

Shay and Dionne are coming
to see you
Umi says from across
the round table
I need you   I need them
to know that you're gonna
make it through
You're gonna make it through, Amal
Just keep going   One foot in front
of the other   Keep walking

LOST-AND-FOUND

And I do
I walk through the program
I walk to the showers

I walk to the mess hall
I walk around my cell
I walk to each of the corners
       with more corners surrounding me
       Kadon, Amir, Smoke, and Rah

I have to put in time
in the mess hall
cleaning tables and washing dishes
Here, they punish you
while punishing you

Then one day
Kadon says
Ay man, come to the library

                Library? I ask

Maybe I'm wrong, but you
look like you know what a library is

he says
He's my shadow
always there   quiet
then he asks
And how come you don't rhyme no more?

               'Cause I don't have shit to say
               no more

Come on, man
There's always some shit to say
We in here   Look, man
it's 'cause you in the mess hall
cleaning up
You gotta earn back some of
that free time so you could
come to that poetry class
Stay on that straight and narrow

Don't fuck up like those
other times

Kadon says
eyes still wandering

Everything he says
makes sense

but the way he's acting
like some shit is ready to pop off
any minute now
doesn't make sense

> *How do you do it, bro?* I ask
> How do you
>   not lose your mind in here?

Kadon laughs
Every day I lose my mind
Every fucking day
But you know what?
I find it again
That's the thing about being
locked up
Whatever you lose
you'll find it again
over and over
You know, like the

lost-and-found at school
Some cardboard box
that all the shit gets dumped into
The shit that people forget
Yeah, we're that box—
a fucking lost-and-found

I laugh a little   for the first time
And whatever stone and brick
that's been inside of me
weighing me down
turns into bubble   turns into air
and floats up and up—
I feel you, man, is all I say

BOOKED II

Even though it's quiet in the library
Things move like
a ticking time bomb
because any minute, some shit will go down
and it always does

The shelves are half empty
and some of the books are so old
just opening them up will make the pages
fall out

I take five books at a time
to a desk, flip open the pages
and wait for my mind
to stop racing
to quiet down
so I can hear the words

I look for an answer
between those pages
I wanna know how I got here
I mean, *really* got here
Like, all the things Uncle Rashon
was telling me about The System

Real talk
I wish Uncle Rashon was here
to give me the right books

Kadon has his head down
and his face in a manga novel

The bookshelves here
are not walls
They're closed windows
and all I have to do
is pull out one book
to make these windows
wide open

FAMILY PORTRAIT III

Shay and Dionne
make a sandwich out of me
They hug me so tight and for so long
that I could've easily slipped
into one of their bags or pockets
and gone home with them

Dang you got skinny, son
Shay says

> *Oh my god, Amal*
> *You're like a different person*
> Dionne says

And it's the first time in a long while
that my eyes get wet
I can't hold back the tears

I knew   I knew
that seeing Shay and Dionne
would make me like a rainstorm

Amal, you're not about to make me
cry in no jail
Shay says

Dionne just lets it all out

Umi is always a quiet rainstorm
by herself

How's college? I ask Dionne

> *A lot of work*, she says
> *You know, studying, adjusting to*
> *a new city, trying to*
> *hold down this part-time job*

She takes my hand and holds it
because she knew   she knew
that her school was in my top three

We can't get Lucas up here 'cause he's not family
But he wants to see you, Shay says
I know   I know
he's lying

Lucas's mom kept him away from me
kept him away from my trial
told him not to text or call me

*Thanks for taking the bus all
the way up here,* is all I say

Best road trip of my life, Shay says
All we did was talk about you

I know y'all were cracking jokes about me
I say

Dionne looks like she's smiling
and crying at the same time

There's an officer with a camera
in front of the kiddie mural
The one with the smiling birds
rainbows and hopping bunnies

There's a short line of guys
with their moms and cousins
and grandmas waiting to take
pictures in front of that mural
like it's picture day in kindergarten

It's the only way they allow photos in here
So Umi, Shay, Dionne, and me

pose in front of the
fading and chipping
mural

I only smile
because I'm with them
and they're here with me

Not for nothing else

When it's time to leave
Umi hugs me so hard and for so long
that I think I'll disappear into her arms

She whispers a line
from her favorite song into my ear
And I have to swallow back
the stone in my throat

When I was little
Umi used to blast Nas
her favorite rapper
and say, *Whose world is this?*
and she would make me sing
It's mine, it's mine, it's mine!

Then she'd play the one with Lauryn Hill
and I'd shout into that musty apartment air
If I ruled the world—
and she'd follow with

I'd free all my sons!

BLANK PAGE II

When I come back to my cell
from the visiting room
there's a notebook
and a box of pencils
on my desk in my cell

There's a juice box
and a bag of potato chips
on my desk in my cell

There's a letter
from Zenobia
on my desk in my cell

I sit on my bed
and stare at those things
as if it's a trick
as if they're poison

but I want them so bad
so bad

So I start with the letter

Dear Amal,

Thanks for the drawing. It's really good. I mean, everybody at school knew you were a dope artist. You forgot to sign your drawing. It'll be worth a lot of money one day. For real. But I'm not going to sell this. I'm framing it and hanging it up in my room.

I heard what they said about you at your trial. People are talking about what Ms. Rinaldi did and it's really messed up. They should've asked one of your friends to be a character witness. I would have done it. I know your character.

You probably don't want to write about what it's like in there and what you're going through. But if you do, I'm here. I'll always write back. Keep your head up.

Zenobia
PS I'm glad you remember me, too. . . .

I fold the letter and
hold it against my chest
where the brick is
where the building is
where the city is

These letters from Zenobia
are putting me back
together again

I slip the letter between the
pages of the notebook
and grab a few pencils
and wait to be let out
for free time in the dayroom

Kadon and the other corners are
at another table
and I don't sit with them on purpose
        I want to be alone here

I don't even get a chance to open my notebook
when Officer Stanford comes to look over my shoulder

        Shahid, is all he says
I start with a line

Amal Shahid, he says
I draw another line, then a box

I don't look up
but he's hovering
like a shadow
          like Tattoo
except his arms are clean

> *You been quiet*, he says
> *Staying out of trouble*
> *It's almost like*
> *you ain't supposed to be here*

I'm not, I mumble

> *It's not up to me*, he says
> *But for now, I see you, Shahid*
> *Keep your head up and head down*
> *at the same time, feel me?*

I look up at him
I look into his eyes this time
and maybe
he's trying to play me
like when I was getting off the bus
So I stare back at him

and wait for
pain

But
Stay low, stay cool, he says
and walks away

and I wonder   I wonder
if anybody else sees what he sees

GUERNICA II

Maybe it was because I'd jumped into
the pages of my sketchbook
drawing boxes around myself
(soundproof steel walls built
with a number two pencil)

that I didn't hear the cursing
the arguing
the fuck-you-niggas
over and over again

By the time I look up
the dayroom
where we play cards
where we bang out beats
on the table
where we eat out of tiny bags
of cookies and potato chips

is a war zone

I get up from my seat
and make my body like steel

eyes watching, jaws clenched
fists ready for any and everything

Then I see Kadon
A guy is beating up
on him so hard and so fast
that I run
leap
jump
and start pulling him off

For each punch, for each blow
I get ten more
on my head
on my back
and my mind shuts down

There's no
thinking in war
I remember
that's how
I got here

The officers run in with their batons
one by one   two by two
we're pulled off
from each other

I'm the first to stop fighting
I keep my hands up

just like that other time
with Omari
But this time in here
I won't let them say
I threw the last punch
I surrendered

I'm frozen
where I stand

innocent

lockdown

THE ENTOMBMENT III

I left my notebook out there
I left my pencils out there
I left Zenobia's letter out there

and even though
it's not nighttime yet

it's lights-out for me

I lay on the cold floor
and curl into myself

like how I was
in Umi's

belly

and slowly   slowly
this tomb
becomes a womb

Here
the darkest night is my canvas

I paint the past in broad strokes, bright hues
And the memories dance all over my mind
in living color

The guys I was skating with
(wearing blue, gray, black, red)
were not trying to get the fuck out

This was our hood, too
even though there
was this invisible line
that separated rich from poor

We were all shades of black
and they were white
no grays
no blurred lines

and ready to deck anybody
who crossed that line
between us and them

and me just standing there
frozen
until   until

I became the color red
boiling-hot lava
rising to the surface

I became a dragon
and the planet Mars

I became
war

I became
rage and revenge

As soon as the first punch went flying
hitting face
hitting belly

as soon as the first soldier went down
hitting pavement
hitting ground

I jumped in

and we were all red
hot bubbling war
We were all a volcano

                              spilling lava
                    all over their side of our hood

          I paint in words and voices, rhymes and rhythm
          and every whisper, every conversation beats a drum
                         in my mind
                         at full blast

Black and white
bodies
turned against each other
lost in the world
thinking it's about money and turf

Light-up in the hood
the tenements and mansions
look pretty now
Bright orange, red, and blue
over a cloud of thick dust
and red-hot heat
Now
this onyx skin
soul made of gold
beautiful and bright
sits in a corner
in a body
trembling and rag-cloaked

I paint in wrong choices, regrets, and broken dreams
and every acquaintance, friend, and enemy laughs at me
in my mind
really, really loud

After that fight with Shawn in the fifth grade
Umi put me in martial arts class

not to learn how to fight
but to learn discipline
and to control my temper

I told her I didn't have a temper
she said, *You will, Amal   you will*

So every Tuesday and Friday
I took the bus to Master John's
basement studio

and I never knew   never knew
that I'd have to use
a karate move
in real life
so close to home
on the other side
of an invisible
line

On a white boy
who said
who said
to my face

Get
the
fuck
off
our
block
nigger

Kadon was beat up real bad in that fight I don't see him

around	and
the	other
corners	Amir
Smoke	and Rah
want	revenge
They	leave me
alone	So with a
new	notebook
I draw	myself
more	boxes
and a	little
black baby	inside

like the one on that officer's arm Except free, inside a box

SAINT PETER IN PRISON

I've been programmed
I get it now

When we know
what we're supposed to do
and when we're supposed to do it
there's no room
for memories
for regret
for fear
for dreams
to slip in

Every single minute of our time
is scheduled
except free time, which isn't free

Except time in our cell
which isn't time
it's hell
when we're left alone
with just our thoughts
our memories
our regret

our fears
our dreams
to slip in
like a sliver of light

So I read and read and read
when there is no blank paper
no blank canvas
to tell this story

I return the books to the library
and I freeze where I'm standing
when I see who's in there

Imani
is standing next to a table
where three other guys are sitting
reading

        Hey, Amal
        she says

And the sun rises
over the city on my chest

        What you been reading?
        Let me see

She takes the books from me
one by one
reading the front and back covers
You have good taste, Amal

I nod
and keep my eye on the other guys

They let me use the library today
for some small-group work
These young men are submitting their
writing to a website
Their words will be read by
thousands of people

That's cool, right?
she says with only her eyes smiling

And I glance at those guys

heads down
typing words into a laptop

I take my books from her
and keep it moving
Hoping that those guys
will leave

so I can ask
if this is something I can do, too

or is this something just
for good behavior

ART SCHOOL II

Today is Tuesday
and we're back in Imani's poetry class

I have a pad
full of drawings and poems
but I won't show her

unless she asks to see them
I hope she asks to see them

We're sitting in a circle
and Imani is across from me
Some other people who are in charge
wearing suits, serious faces, and badges
stand outside the circle, watching
including Cheryl-Ann Buford

A man walks in behind them
wearing jeans and a dashiki
A shiny chain and medallion hangs
from his neck
He has on a bunch of rings and bracelets, too
and I wonder   I wonder

why on earth did they let him walk in here
with all that ice

The other people look as if they're parting
a sea for him
and he glides, almost like Imani
to the front of the dayroom

smiling as if we're all his sons
and he's seeing us
for the first time

Then Imani says
I am so excited for you to meet
our very special guest today

Everybody shifts in their seat
I sit up and inhale

It is a tremendous honor
to introduce Dr. Kwesi Bennu

We clap only because we're supposed to
I've never heard of him before

He steps in front of us
and says

Over thirty years ago
I was exactly where you are now
Accused, tried, and convicted
spending six years in jail
for a crime I did not commit

I sit up taller
because everything—
time   the air   and maybe my heart—
stops for a moment
as we listen to his story

It was summertime
and like most of you
I didn't want to be
stuck in the house

I rolled with my boys
like most of you do
And I don't ever
want you to think
there's something
wrong with that

Your boys are
like family out on
these streets

But you gotta understand
when one of you fall
everybody falls
or takes the fall
You know what I'm saying?

I didn't rob that grocery store
I didn't have a weapon on me

But it was a matter of
wrong time, wrong place

But wrong time, wrong place
doesn't make you
automatically guilty

I'm sure you all know
the rule of law—
Innocent until proven guilty

But with us, it's
guilty until proven innocent

I served six years
before I was proven innocent

HARMONY

We don't write
instead, we tell our stories
out loud
for everyone to hear

Our voices bounce off the walls
and it almost sounds like a rap battle
and maybe if there was some dope beat
behind all our truths
it would be the dopest collaboration
in hip-hop history

If only somebody would listen
and Dr. Bennu and Imani
and those people in suits
listen to us

> *I took a plea deal*

> *They told me I was*
> *going back home, too*

> *We couldn't afford a lawyer*

I was there, I did it
but I didn't know it was going
to end up like that

They said I'd serve less time
if I said I did it

Sometimes I get so mad and
I don't know how to fucking
calm down

If I didn't do it, they'd kill me

It was gonna be me or him

I needed the money

I wasn't even there

I didn't think I'd get caught

It's the only life I know

I didn't do it

AFRICAN AMERICAN II

While we talk   shout   whisper
Imani writes on her poster board

THE 13TH AMENDMENT

Then she writes some more words

Dr. Bennu nods
Y'all should know this, he says
Y'all should really understand this

Constitution of the United States of America

Thirteenth Amendment

Section 1

Neither slavery nor involuntary servitude, except as a punishment for crime whereof the party shall have been duly convicted, shall exist within the United States, or any place subject to their jurisdiction.

Section 2

Congress shall have power to enforce this article by appropriate legislation.

Dr. Bennu tells us to
read each word out loud

We bitch and moan
moan and bitch
Nobody wants to
but I do

So we're like slaves?
I ask

Is that what it says?
Dr. Bennu asks

Basically, if we've been
convicted of a crime
we're slaves

So when you did whatever you did
or whatever they think you did
Your life   your whole damn life
belongs to them

Now read what it says
on those orange jumpsuits

You've been branded
labeled   boxed in
You've become property
of the state

     Tell us something we don't know!
     I blurt out

Some of the guys laugh
but Dr. Bennu and Imani
and all the other
important people in suits
stare at me

You're right, youngblood
Dr. Bennu says
You don't belong to anyone
while you're in here
Not even to yourself
And you already know that

He's about to leave
and the words are
caught in my throat
stuck there
like stone

Excuse me, Dr. Bennu, I say
standing from my seat

I swallow back
the stone
and make my fist a mic

I make truth out of the air
out of the room
out of this place

Saying down with the blacks but uplift the white race
Raising the banner to the sun in haste
Mobbed deep, hoods and capes
Sun-dried and bloodstained
Saying down with the blacks but uplift the white race

Unjustly tried an indelible conviction
the usual result of five shades of darker skin
Justice unjust, black robes and pale face

Didn't have a chance, they called us apes
I wish I would have known the false smiles
Evil intentions fulfilling their taste
Why me?   Why us?
Justice unjust, black robes and pale face

BUTTERFLIES

Do you know why you're in here?
Dr. Bennu asks, stepping closer to me
I mean, why you're really in here?

He steps back to look at everyone else

All those stories you just told me
is a truth   your truth
but it's not the whole truth

Of course, you're here to take
responsibility for your actions, but—

> *But what if we didn't do it?*
> *What if we have no actions to be*
> *responsible for?* I ask

> *What if we took a fucking plea deal?*
> somebody else asks

Dr. Bennu pauses
looks at us for a long minute
then asks
Is there any paper here?

Imani hands him a stack
of loose-leaf paper
and I'm thinking I could use
some myself

Then Dr. Bennu takes some sheets
and tears them into big pieces

Each of you, he says
*Take a piece of paper
and write down one thing
you are guilty of
one thing you regret*

                    A mistake, Imani reminds us

*That's right   A mistake
It could be anything,* he says
*Including the thing you did
or didn't do to get here*

We shift in our seats again
We bitch and moan some more

                    *Why you wanna know?
                    You're gonna use this
                    against us*

I need my lawyer

And then we write anyway
one by one   two by two
we all start writing something
down on paper
slowly
as if each word is a secret

          Mine is:

          I
          threw
          the
          first
          punch

Dr. Bennu looks around the dayroom
and grabs an empty trash can
Take that piece of paper
fold it up real small
and throw it into this bin

We all do what he says

Now I'll go around and you
have to pick out one piece of paper

We complain some more

I remember what Kadon had said
In here, we are a lost-and-found

We try to forget something
throw it away
but we can always dig it back up
when we're ready
because it's still here   trapped
just like us

And something hits me deep in my belly
                    Kadon isn't here

Put it back in if you pick your own paper
Dr. Bennu says

My piece of paper
which isn't my piece of paper
which isn't my mistake
says

Being born

He tells us all
to read the mistake out loud

He calls it our mistake
but it isn't our mistake
it's someone else's mistake

But holding it in our hands like this
seeing the words on paper like this
reading it out loud like this

it becomes our mistake

How can being born
be a mistake?

How can your whole life
be something you wish didn't happen?

Imani writes our mistakes
down on her poster board
for everyone to read
for everyone to see

Mine is there
naked   exposed   raw

   I threw the first punch

The one I read is there, too

   Being born

I look around wondering which one of us
thinks   believes   that they are a mistake

DNA II

Dr. Bennu tells us to get up from our chairs—
—and stand next to each other—
—Then he tells us to lock arms at the elbows—
—and we look like we're chained to each other—
—in a circle arm in arm—
—He walks outside of our circle, then—
—one by one and two by two—
—he starts to push each one of us forward—
—He keeps pushing and pushing until—
—we hold on to each other so tight that—
—when he pushes again, we don't fall—
—we don't stumble—
—We are a chain link like DNA strands—

-U-N-B-R-E-A-K-A-B-L-E-

CONVERSATIONS WITH GOD IX

Dr. Bennu doesn't come every day
Imani doesn't come every day

So as soon as those metal doors shut
as soon as the buzzer goes off
as soon as it's lights-out

and lights on
and program begins

it's the same shit
over and over again
day in day out

We forget all about the lessons
or maybe
the lessons don't stick
don't land
don't sink to the bottom of our souls

Dr. Bennu's words
only skim the surface of our skins
So with the markers
I copped from Imani

I write down his words
to remember—

When she had asked me
to help her put away her stuff

When she turned her back
the markers were
just sitting there on a table

I grabbed all of them
and stuffed them into
my jumpsuit

I felt them drop to the bottom
almost slipping out
over the top of my sneakers

So you're a poet, she asked
I nodded
I wanted to say more
I wanted to spit some more rhymes
I wanted to tell her that I
paint and draw, too

but the markers—

What you did there
was fire
I like your metaphors
and similes and imagery
she said

and all I did was shrug
because the markers—

She turned away again
digging in her bag for something
and I bent over to tuck the bottom
of my jumpsuit into my sneakers
keeping the markers in place

lights out

BLANK CANVAS II

The best thoughts swim around
your mind when you're locked up
in a box with nothing but the
quiet darkness and cool concrete walls
as your canvas

I'm thinking about Zenobia

so the first thing I draw
is a butterfly

the curved lines of its wings
in flight
fluttering in the air
changing the movement
of atoms and molecules
shifting the tiniest cells
the smallest, most irrelevant truths
so that one big thing can happen
way on the other side of this wall
of this cell
of this prison

Then I write

I THREW THE FIRST PUNCH

It was me who stepped to him first
It was me who balled up my fist
and hit him so hard he went

stumbling but not falling
he caught himself
and came back for me

The look in his eyes
I knew   I knew
he wanted to destroy me

And the other guys around me
were going to war

People started
coming out of their houses
somebody had a bat
somebody yelled
I'm calling the cops!
Somebody threw that word

around again
nigger
nigger
nigger
like it's the fucking 1950s

It echoed
bounced off the houses
reached the sky
landed on the pavement

and it wasn't even the word
that made us run for our lives
made me leave my skateboard

made me climb over a gate
almost fall flat on my face
mess up my hands and knees

made me double over
trying hard to catch my breath
made me sit on a curb

when I wasn't even home yet
so that those cops
pull up right in front of me

lights blazing
guns drawn
rushing to me as if

I was about to make them chase me
when all I was doing was

catching my breath
catching my breath
catching my breath

Even while they pushed
me to the ground and
shoved my face
against the pavement
pulled my hands behind
my back

handcuffed
handcuffed
handcuffed

and threw me into the back seat
threw me into a room
with a table and chair
as I whispered
as I said

It was a fight!
It was a fight!

IT WAS JUST A FUCKING FIGHT

I write this
on the wall
in giant letters

It's so dark
I can't even see
where my words land

I don't even know
who is hearing this drawing
through the silence

lights on

The walls
the floor
the desk
my sheets
my hands

are all covered in
red, black, and green
ink

Tattoo
is the first one
to come to my door
and see what I've done

Tattoo

grabs me from
off my bed
throws me to
the ground
handcuffs me

and hisses in my ear

What did Stanford tell you
when you first got here?
No celebrities in here
No fucking special treatment
or else
we can arrange that

Get off me!
I shout
Get the fuck off me!

solitary: the box

SURREALISM

I ball myself up
At least in here
no one will hear
me cry for Umi

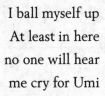

At least in here
I can spit rhymes
as loud as I want
I can curse the air

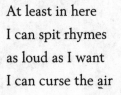

At least in here
I can see the butterfly
I drew on my wall
make its way into this box

fluttering around my head
as if telling me a secret
as if affecting something
way on the other side of this box

If I could change one thing
about that night
I wouldn't even know where
to start and where to end

Maybe all the decisions
all the mistakes
I've made were supposed
to lead me right to this moment

Butterfly, you mean to tell me
that everything I've ever done
in all my sixteen years of living
were just so I could end up here?

Butterfly
what about my dreams
what about all that work
I did just to stay alive?

Butterfly, why are you even in here?
What are you supposed to be changing?
Maybe there's already a shift
Us and them

                              I don't know if I'll change
                                 I've been so broken
                                too many times that I
                                have turned to dust

Butterfly, you'd have to promise me
you'll change them out there, too
It can't be just me
They gotta be different, too

                              They gotta listen this time
                                when I say that I didn't
                                 throw the last punch
                                    It wasn't me

It wasn't me
who left
Jeremy Mathis
for dead
It wasn't me
who threw that last
fatal blow
to the head
making him lose
consciousness
making him fall into
an in-between space
where he can't even
tell the truth
about what happened that night

I threw the first punch
but I didn't throw the last
It wasn't me

IT WASN'T ME!

Butterfly, if you could do just one thing for me

listen to us
listen to all of us

When we say
When I say
that I was tired
of them
acting like
they own that block
that side of our hood
our city
our country
our world

When we say
When I say
that maybe
I was punching
all the walls
they put up around me
around us

I was punching
the air
the clouds
the sun

for pressing
down on me

on us
so hard
that the weight
of the world
made us crack
split in half
break into pieces

and Jeremy Mathis

and all those white boys
that night
were like the air

Just by them standing there
being there
living there
claiming what's not theirs

We couldn't breathe
I couldn't breathe

Butterfly, if what they say is true about you
change something BIG out there

Butterfly, remind me again what happens to dust

Butterfly, if you're in here with me
then you have to go back out there
and change the world

I made you, butterfly

The butterfly swirls and swirls
down to the cold concrete floor

It flutters its wings faster and faster
so fast that two wings become four

and a second butterfly joins it
Four wings become eight wings

Eight wings become sixteen
become thirty-two fluttering wings

And right here in this box
right in front of my eyes

butterflies fill this space and
circle around each other until

a pair of old sneakers appears in
the middle of their butterfly dance

In the middle of their cypher
a pair of legs comes out of the sneakers

jeans, a shirt, arms, shoulders, a head
A whole man appears just as the

butterflies disappear
I rub my eyes, close and open them

to make sure that what I'm seeing
is what I'm seeing

Baba? I say

Assalaamu alaikum

I stand to face him
and he's smiling the same way

he did for my elementary school
graduation—proud and happy

> *Amal, my son—*
> *Wa alaikum assalaam*
> my baba says

and his voice fills the room
and pushes against the walls

as if it's too big for this place
like man-sized feet in kid-sized shoes

There's not even enough room for my voice
and I can't find the right words

to say all the things I wanted to say
but all I can ask is

Baba, do you know what happened?
Do you know what happened to me?
Did somebody call you?
Did you see me on the news?
Did you, Baba, did you?

> *Amal,* he says
> *I want you to know that not*
> *a day goes by*
> *that I don't regret not telling*
> *you something*
> *not showing you something—*
> *Amal, I want you to know*
> *that there's just so much*
> *so so much in the world that*
> *you don't know*
> *that you need to know*

and I don't know   I didn't
know
where to even start—

And I shouldn't have blinked
I shouldn't have taken a breath
because in that small moment
when it's dark
when I'm exhaling
when I'm breathing

he's gone again

lights on

BROTHERHOOD III

I don't even have to
read the name
on the envelope

to know who it's from
The handwriting is a
dead giveaway

We're both juniors
and his handwriting
hasn't changed since

kindergarten   Lucas
is no artist   He
was never good at

drawing   But
he was good with
the girls   We

called him Pretty Boy
Luc 'cause that's all
he cared about

His drip, his swag, his girls

And part of me
doesn't even want to
open the envelope

Reading anything
from him will make me
want to be home

But it's already been open
The guards search these
envelopes and even though

they're not supposed to
read our letters
I think they do

And I wonder
what Lucas has to say
after all this time

For Amal's eyes only!!!

Yo I can't believe you got me writing letters!!! I don't even do that for my girl.

Well this ain't a fucking letter, this is a fucking note. Just pretend I passed you this note in class or something. And all I gotta say is my mom was tripping. If it wasn't for her, I would've been there. She was just worried, that's all. This whole shit is fucked up. I mean, from day one. I can't come see you 'cause we're not blood and that shit is fucked up, too. If I could, I would. That's my word. But I know you're good in there. You're probably drawing and reciting poetry. Don't let them stop you, though. Your shit is nice. I told you that. Keep your head up. I know that when this whole shit blows over, AND IT WILL, you're gonna be mad famous. I'm gonna see your name in lights, homie. Just keep doing your thing.

Luc

PS That girl Zenobia was asking about you. I told her she should just write you.

I fold his letter
really small
and hold it
in my hand

Smiling and remembering
all the dumb shit
me and Lucas used to do

Like that one time
he just showed up at my
school even though

he wasn't a student there
all because he wanted
to shoot his shot with some girl

He came to my classes
and everything and just
sat there answering questions

and doing the work
and I couldn't stop laughing
Yo that shit was mad funny

And I was the one
to get in trouble
for laughing   Not him

I still couldn't stop
laughing even while sitting
in the principal's office

and he poked his head in
talking about, *You're good, homie?*

Yo! I wanted to blurt

*Nigga, you don't even
go to this school!*
But I didn't

I wanted to hang
with him that night
But I didn't

Lucas wouldn't have gone
to that park that night
But I did

BROTHERHOOD IV

I press my face
against the glass
on the door to my cell

looking out into
the dayroom
for a pencil
a pen, a marker

anything
so I can
write Lucas back

and Zenobia
and Umi
and Grandma
and Shay and Dionne

And that's when I see him
      Kadon
His back turned to me
hunched over
head down

as if they forced all the life
out of him

He's handcuffed
and Tattoo is holding his arm
and my stomach sinks

I wanna see Kadon's face
I wanna see if it's still there
the same crooked smile
eyes bright
looking as if this is not
the worst thing that's ever
happened to him

A smile
that says that it could be worse
it could all be much worse

So I

BANG and BANG and BANG and BANG

Tattoo turns to face my door
but Kadon doesn't

It's Stanford who shows up
in my door's window

                              and asks
                              What you need, Shahid?

I lick my lips
thinking of something to say
or to ask so that he could let me out
to talk to Kadon
before Tattoo walks away with him

So I just ask
What's up with my man Kadon?

                              Ay, yo, Williams!
                              Stanford calls out
                              to Kadon

But Tattoo pulls him away

but I
BANG and BANG and BANG and BANG

Yo, chill!
Stanford says

Kadon! I call out
through the closed metal door
I need to see his face
I need to see what they did to him
Kadon!

And finally   finally
he looks up
even as Tattoo pulls him
and just about drags
him out of the dayroom
He looks up and toward my door
and I see his face

like
a pink balloon ready to burst

his bottom lip hangs so low
that it almost touches his chin

and
one eye is sealed shut
swollen glossy

and
I wonder   I wonder
if there's even an eye there
anymore

Kadon trips and Tattoo drags him
Kadon doesn't fight

So I
BANG and BANG and BANG and BANG

> *There's nothing you can do*
> *Shahid*
> Stanford says
> and walks away

And I scream
through that small
glass window
hoping
hoping that
it will
shatter

BROTHERHOOD V

Questions not to ask while in juvie:

What you in here for?

Do I know you?

Who did that to you?

You a'ight, man? I ask Kadon
a few days later when I see him
in the mess hall

He's smaller now
as if whatever happened to him—
whatever they did to him—
pressed down on him so hard
that he's half the boy he used to be

I sit up taller for both of us
until I have to leave him there

but it feels like I lost him
and I won't be able to find him anymore

Kadon was wrong
You can lose something, everything, in here

CONVERSATIONS WITH GOD X

Care to tell me why you were
screaming in your cell
the other day, Amal?
Cheryl-Ann Buford asks

Being in her office
is like going to see the
principal, the guidance counselor
the social worker, the teacher
all at once

Keep thinking this is a game
and you'll be doubling your
sentence
Before you know it, you'll
spend half your
life in the system
I know your type, Amal
You think the world owes you
something
You think you're innocent
and you don't deserve to be
here
But guess what?

You're here now
and you're not going
  anywhere
anytime soon, so do what
  you need to do—

She says those last words
  like she's my mother
She's not   She's not

I let her hear the sound of her own
voice echo for a second before I ask
What happened to Kadon?

Worry about yourself
  she says
as she types on her
  keyboard
and fills out another form
like it's her actual job—
writing report cards for us

Who brought that man here—
Dr. Bennu?
I ask
He made us write our mistakes down
and then we had to read

somebody else's mistake
That meant something, right?
We were doing something
that made us think differently—
at least I know I did

But you're over here
being the judge and jury
when that's not even your job—

> *Excuse me?*
> *Who do you think you're*
> *talking to?*

What are you gonna tell
Kadon's mother and father
about what happened to him?

> She folds her hands across
> her desk and leans in

But before she can say anything
I get up to leave

BUTTERFLIES II

I need to
make it to
Tuesday
for poetry

so I turn
myself into
a wall

and become
brick
metal
concrete
and sharp
corners

Here   walls   don't   break
Someone   someone
returned Zenobia's second letter
and my notebook
and one pencil
I open to a blank page
and for the first time
I don't know what words

to write

I don't know what lines
to bend into curves and shapes

so I start with her name

Zenobia Angel Garrett

and even as the lights go out

I draw myself a girlfriend

I start with what I remember the most
Zenobia's eyes
then her long blue braids
then
her angel wings

and I wish   I wish
she would come alive from off my page

just like my father did
from off the wall

And she does

There's a breeze in the room
all of a sudden

It's an angel's wings
come to wrap around me like warm arms

Her eyes light up the darkness
and we hold hands

Then I hug her and pull her close, close
and it's just me and my angel girlfriend
made of soft charcoal lines
curved and rounded
at just
the right
places

ART SCHOOL III

We don't write
during Imani's poetry class

I missed the last few days
when they had an open mic

I was stuck in the mess hall
for what I did to the wall

and I notice that a bunch of guys
I hadn't seen before are in here

Poetry class is voluntary

but only the black and brown kids
were here   And now
we're like colorful markers

bleeding over the lines

Still, everybody sits on their side of the dayroom
but Imani keeps going as if she doesn't see
the white boys sneering at her
She hands out loose-leaf and pencils

and this is when—
while we're waiting for directions
while we're waiting for her to tell us
      where the pencil point should land
      where the first word should leave its mark
      how our truth should look on the page
      how our memories should sound off the page—
that the words want to pour out of me so bad   so bad
that I start to write

Dear Zenobia,

I wanted to shoot my shot so many times, but I didn't
want to look stupid. I didn't want you to diss me. I
thought you thought I was ugly. I know this will sound
corny, but whoever named you Angel—

Amal—
would you like to share your writing?
Imani asks

I'm caught off guard
I read the words I just
wrote over to myself—

I don't want to force you
but
I know you like to share
your rhymes
And I want all of you to know
that there's no failing in art
There is no wrong art
There is no bad art
Just art
Just your truth—
she says

I pause for a second
thinking of Ms. Rinaldi
who failed me
over and over again
No failing in art, huh? I say
A'ight then

I lick my lips, swallow hard
and
read the words that were
supposed to be
for Zenobia's eyes only
to these guys out loud

and they laugh
and they say

You sound too desperate—
Tell her to send some nudes—
Can you write me a letter to send to my girl?

and they laugh
and I laugh—

Imani laughs, too

BROTHERHOOD VI

And maybe
there are small
cracks in our walls
and we start to see
a sliver of light
shine through

in each other

Some of you wrote down your mistakes
when Dr. Bennu was here
Imani says
Now, let's write down our misgivings
our gut feelings, our deep intuitions
Those whispers you hear in

the back of your mind
but ignore
before your mistakes happen—
Misgivings

> My paper stays blank
> *Misgivings don't matter,* I say

Well, did you have any? she asks
Forewarnings, premonitions?
A moral compass trying
to point you in the right direction?

> *Yeah—that's why they don't*
> *matter*
> *I'm still here*

But, still
some of us write them down

put them into the trash
where we dig them back up
and read each other's words
out loud
as if they're our own

My mother told me to come right home—

        My next-door neighbor said to stay away
        from those guys—

        My older brother told me not to fuck with them
        niggas—

                I stopped to get one more
                thing from the store—

Something wasn't right about how they were looking at us—

        I was supposed to pick my little sister up
        from school—

        I was supposed to be somewhere else, with someone
        else, doing something else—

I wanted to be here, so I followed my gut
I didn't misgive nothing—

Imani grabs a chair and sits close to us
She folds her hands over her lap
and this is the first time I'm seeing her
really seeing her

Her face holds secrets
Her eyes could be both young and old
and she's dead serious right now

> I learned so much from you
> all, she says

and I sit up in my seat because
the way she says this—

> Brothers, this is my last day
>   here, but
> I'm just getting started—
> I'm so inspired to go out there
>   and do the work
> of talking to those young
>   brothers and sisters out
>   there—
> of tearing down this system
>   from the top—
> So what should I tell them?
> How should I talk to your

> brothers and sisters
> so we can end this cycle?
> What should I say to
> policy makers, heads of
> corporations
> anybody who's making a
> dime off you being here?

What do you mean? I ask
What do you want us to do?

> Give me something to take
> back out there—

But we need you in here
I say

> And they need me out there
> too, she says

And it hits me like
a punch to my gut

ART SCHOOL IV

You said you wanted to see my poetry
well here it is—

You said you would give me feedback
tell me if my words matter in here—

You said that we are each other's
mistakes and misgivings—

Tell me why when you leave
it's like you were never here—

Tell me why they bring you in here
and take you away so fast—

The other guys are gone
and Imani asked the officer
who was supposed to take me
back to my cell
if I could help her pack

She only has a few spare notebooks
and some markers

She sees me eyeing them

> *I know how you feel, Amal—*
> *I love this work, trust*
> *But a five-hour bus ride from*
>   *the city*
> *is hard for me*
> *And I don't even know if I'm*
> *making a difference*
> *But the fact that you're here*
> *asking all these questions*
> *I know that*
> *I mattered to you—*

There's nothing more she can
say to me now
so I start to leave

> *Wait,* she says
> *I really don't want you*
> *getting me*
> *in trouble again for leaving*
>   *markers out*
> *So come with me to Ms.*
>   *Buford's office*
> *I got something I want you*
>   *to see*

Cheryl-Ann Buford isn't in her office
but Imani has the keys

She opens up the door and pulls
out a taped-up box that was sitting by her desk

She picks it up but I rush to help her

> *We're taking this to the*
> *Visiting Room*
> she says

Tattoo appears in the doorway
and my stomach sinks
He keeps his eyes on me without helping

I peep Imani glancing at him
Then she rolls her eyes
as if she knows
Maybe she's seen it
      that tattoo

We stand in front of that mural—
the one with the chipping paint
and happy, singing birds

The one that's supposed to remind us
that we are juveniles
kids
children
even though everything else
lets us know that they think we are fully grown
that we've already become everything we're
supposed to be

Imani opens the box
and in it are cans of paint
six colors in all
with paintbrushes in different sizes

I had put in an order for
    these supplies
months ago, but they're just
    getting here
now that I'm leaving
That's why I hate this
    bureaucratic bullshit

Y'all were supposed to
    repaint that mural
It was supposed to be a
group project
I had to jump through all
    kinds of hoops
to get this approved
I guess this was
their way of saying no
    without saying no
to my face   Feel me?

Listen, Amal
I saw what you drew on
your wall
and what it meant to you
I don't want that talent
that gift
to go to waste in here
I want you to paint over that
ugly-ass mural
Paint your truth, Amal—
And get those guys to
help you

This feels like
 like growing wings
 like flying

I look at Imani
She looks at me waiting
for an answer
and
there's nothing left to do
but to drop down next to that box
and break out of myself
 open the doors to myself
 wide open

and fly   and fly
and paint

and I know   I know
that this time
my punches will land on a wall
my punches will be paintbrushes

The largest canvas
Ms. Rinaldi
ever let me paint on
was a six by nine—

And even then—
        when I'd studied
        the Sistine Chapel
        and all of Michelangelo's paintings
        and dreamed of having my work
        in some fancy place
        like the Louvre in Paris
        and dreamed of painting
        the ceiling of a giant mosque
        and memorized all the works
        of Picasso and Salvador Dalí
        Rembrandt and Van Gogh

Monet, da Vinci, and Matisse—
my art was wrong, according to her

Even though my subjects were soft and tender
she didn't think it was my truth

Be honest with yourself, she said

I was
I was being honest
I was telling the truth

No one had ever given me
a whole wall for a canvas
to tell my truth

AMERICAN GRAFFITI

So instead of following the program
I get Kadon
Amir, Smoke, and Rah
to help me sketch out the mural

Imani made sure to get approval
from Cheryl-Ann Buford
It's the least she could do
since the supplies arrived so late

Stanford
will be the officer
in charge

Still
the next morning
I start prepping the wall
while the Four Corners
are in the mess hall

No one is here to watch me
for now
and in this moment

I am free

I should've been painting that night
or sketching or thinking or reading

but my home was starting to feel like a box
My room was starting to feel like a box

The home that I've known all my life
was squeezing in around me

forcing me to be small, small
when all I was doing was growing tall

Growing too wide for all the boxes around me
Umi couldn't contain me anymore

I wanted to get the fuck out
push back walls

so that I could

punch the air
make an opening
wide and tall enough
for me to step in

                                              and fly
                                          and soar

I draw myself
I draw Kadon
I draw Imani
I draw Dr. Bennu
I draw Amir, Smoke, and Rah
I draw wings

All of us with wings

we fly we fly we fly

Above all the chaos
below
is a remix of my
favorite painting
          Guernica, by Pablo Picasso
with its distorted faces and bodies
in war   in war   in war

But like dust
                              we rise
              we rise
we rise

BROTHERHOOD VII

Kadon, Amir, Smoke, and Rah
help me paint

We crack jokes
and clown each other
and the wings I drew
them are actually there
on their backs

We paint
and we fly

Even Stanford
who's standing guard
        clowns us
talking about
        Y'all can't even stay in the lines
        on a fucking drawing
        No wonder y'all can't even walk
        in a straight line

The other guys clown us
for not being in class
talking about

Y'all niggas get to do
a fucking art project?

But still
they leave us alone

Even when we have
to leave the mural unfinished
for the next day
they leave it alone

It takes us a whole week
to finish

but I'm left alone
to add some final touches
here and there
and I stand back
to look at my work

our work—

YOUNG BASQUIAT

At some point
I stopped caring about Ms. Rinaldi's
Advanced Placement Art History class

But Umi got on me for
cutting class

Amal, you love art
You know this stuff
Why are you being so
        so defeatist?

Umi didn't know
that I had cut school
to visit the art museum downtown
        I had cut school
to sit in the park
on a bench with my sketch pad

drawing trees and leaves
and sky and birds

just to get my skills up

just to understand the rules
        of line and texture
        and shading
and
black and white

Just so I can break those rules

And I didn't need Ms. Rinaldi
to tell me that I wasn't advanced
or I didn't have history

There, outside of my arts high school
the internet was my teacher
and
I discovered
Jacob Lawrence and Romare Bearden
Faith Ringgold and Kerry James Marshall
Alma Thomas and Norman Lewis

So when
the mural is
finally done
and it's Visitors Day
and the guys start
coming to the dayroom

and the families
start lining up to take
pictures in front of it

Kadon says
with the widest smile
I've seen on him
in weeks
> *That's fire, son!*
> *Young Basquiat, for real!*

The heavy thing in my throat
falls out onto the floor and disappears

The heavy thing on my chest
rises out of my body and disappears

I get applause when the guys see it
I get pats on the back, daps, handshakes
I get respect because I did something
that I wanted to do even while trapped

in this box

THE PERSISTENCE OF MEMORY II

It's my turn
to see Umi
on Visitors Day

The walls here
are pushed back farther
The lights here
shine brighter

Me and some of the others guys
I don't know
start cracking jokes
and we're laughing more

I'm laughing more

Umi gets to see what I've done
and we'll take a picture

The families of the other
inmates will take pictures
in front of my masterpiece, too

but

my name isn't called
to go into the Visiting Room

Umi can't be late
She's never been late
or else
she won't get to see me

She won't get to see my wall
and
I'm called into the room
with the pay phones instead
and
it's not like Umi to call
when she's supposed to be here
        She's supposed to be here

and

He's out of the coma, Amal
Umi says on the other line
without explaining why she isn't here
Jeremy Mathis is awake—

Jeremy Mathis is awake?
I repeat
just to make sure that I
  heard her right
Did he start talking?
Did he remember what
  happened?

Amal—
I have to be here in case
he starts talking
I have to make sure that
they record the truth
If his words are the key
that will unlock the door
to your freedom

Amal—

I hang up the phone
and freeze where I'm standing
like a statue
Time stands still
and in this moment
only Jeremy Mathis's words
will turn me from stone
to human

Let's go, Shahid!
an officer's words
force me to move

I join the line

walking back to our cells

I look into the Visiting Room
to get a glance at my mural
and
that's when I see him

Tattoo

standing there
with his arms crossed
head tilted back
checking out
my mural

MEDITATION II

A letter on my desk
in my cell
lets me know that
I am human
lets me know that

I feel   I feel   I feel

Dear Amal,

Please don't laugh at my drawing of you. I didn't go online to find a picture or nothing. I drew you from memory, from how I saw you at school. You. The real you.

Zenobia

BROTHERHOOD VIII

In the mess hall
Kadon comes to sit next to me

The bandages on his face are off
The swelling has gone down

But there's something else written on his face
and I stare at him trying to read his eyes

He's shaking mad

Who? I ask

It's gone, he whispers
The whole thing is gone

AMERICAN GRAFFITI II

My mural
with its sharp angles and straight lines
turned into
black curved and rounded lines
turned into
black curved and rounded
wings and faces

is painted over

         in white
         in white
         in white

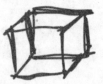

YOUNG BASQUIAT II

So I make myself a world
I make myself a border
I make myself a people

and become war
and become hate
and become oppression
and become a box
and become a wall

and—

Kadon comes over to me
wraps his arms around me
in a bear hug
Calm down, Young Basquiat
Calm the fuck down—
There are more walls here
We got nothing but fucking walls here—

I b r e a k

They said my mural
was against the facility's guidelines

No gang colors, signs, or symbols

and all I could do
was hold my head
in my hands
and whisper under my breath

Fuck you!

What the fuck were we
supposed to do with that paint then?
Draw more cartoons?
More smiling birds and a winking sun?
Paint more lies?

FATHER FIGURE

Umi's face was never
a mirror for me

If she cried when she saw me
during Visitors Day

I knew that her tears
told me nothing about how

messed up my face is
how skinny I got

how dirty or depressed or angry I look

But it's Uncle Rashon's eyes
that hold a mirror up to me
when he finally visits
and I finally walk up to him
that almost break me
into smaller pieces

Right there in front of my uncle
the man who tried to take my father's place

I become dust and almost get blown away
only to land right back where I am
because
this is a box

I'm not here to feel sorry for you, Amal—
Uncle Rashon says

He's wearing a kufi and dashiki
as if my being here has woken him up
to the injustices in the world

> *I don't want you to feel sorry*
> *for me*
> I say

That's not what I mean, Amal—
I mean, your mother will do that for you
and your grandmother and Dionne
But when you see me walk up in here
after driving for five hours
know that I had a lot to think about—

He reaches into his bag and pulls out
a stack of books
They can't lock down your mind, Amal—
only if you let them

Your mind is free
Your thoughts are free
Your creativity is free—

Behind him is the white wall
where my mural used to be
I didn't even take a picture of it

> *I know, I say*
> *But, why are you*
> *showing your face now?*
> *You had all this time*
> *to bring me books*

If I didn't take all that time, Amal
I would've   I would've—
he swallows hard as if
there's a stone in his throat, too

> Then I just say
> *Thanks for coming, Unc*

> The first book in his stack
>   is called
> *The Mis-Education*
> *of the Negro*
> and it's by Carter G. Woodson

The next books are by
James Baldwin
Richard Wright
Toni Morrison
Octavia Butler
Ibram X. Kendi
Michelle Alexander
and Ta-Nehisi Coates

Next time I come
we'll discuss what you've read—
he says before leaving

and it's the first time Uncle Rashon
has ever hugged me

BROTHERHOOD IX

Kadon is with me in the library
and he grabs
a James Baldwin book from my pile

Me and Kadon—
who is quiet, pensive, drained—
start with one book
     one page
     one word

as if each idea is a link on a chain
that we are breaking
     one by one
     and two by two

I slide a blank paper and a pencil to Kadon
     He reads, then he draws
     straight lines at first   He makes himself a grid

I take a paper and copy entire paragraphs from the books
so that piece of truth can carve its way into my soul
one word at a time

I read, then I draw
curved lines at first
rounding out the dark, sharp corners
bending the straight lines
        until I make myself a circle and
        another and another

and like from a round belly
I push myself out
        eyes bright
        barely crying
                I am born again
                into this old   old soul

WALLFLOWER III

It's Tattoo
who comes to my cell
to tell me to get out

>   *Shahid! You got a phone call*
>   *Let's go!*
>   he shouts purposely into my ear
>   as I walk past him and out of my cell

I can't even look at his face
But he is like the walls here
      like the metal and bars
He and everything he stands for
is part of The System—

HOPE IV

Umi says
on the other side
of that phone line

Amal—
I fired Mr. Richter
He did the best he could
But I don't think his best
was good enough for you   for us
I decided it was time

for a new attorney
         Someone who gets it
         who gets us, you know?

Her name is
Tarana Hudson

                    I wasn't performing Salat
                    like Umi told me to
                    I wasn't praying five times a day
                    to ask Allah to show me a way
                    But this   this
                    this is a wall crumbling down

Why? I ask her

Amal, I'm in her office now
and I'll let her tell you

> Mr. Shahid
> Tarana Hudson
> says on the other side
> of that phone line
>
> *I've been following your case*
> *since the very beginning and*
> *I've been getting to know you*
>   *Amal*
> *through your mother*
> *I know you're a good kid*
> *and it's an honor*
> *to work with you and*
> *your family*
> *Amal, I want you to*
> *know that*
>
> *Jeremy Mathis*
> *is ready to talk—*

BUTTERFLIES III

Kadon is sitting
across from me
in the dayroom

Amir, Smoke, and Rah
are there, too—
Corners

Snacks are thrown
all over the tables
but I don't care
because
I miss Umi's
lamb and rice

No one has come
to replace Imani
and her poetry workshops

No one has come
to inspire us
like Dr. Bennu

But someone put
construction paper
and crayons on the tables

like this is kindergarten
The Four Corners
start playing cards

and I'm a fifth wheel
Not even a corner in a box
Just me

Amal

taking up space in the
middle of nowhere

Hope
taking up space in the
middle of nowhere
The crayons are even more broken
as if someone knew
that I'm the only one
in here
who uses them like that

I try to find a whole one
enough to hold
between my long fingers

I see Stanford looking
at me from across the room

I keep drawing
even as the crayon
crumbles between my fingers

YOUNG BASQUIAT III

We're walking back
from the mess hall
        straight line
        hands behind our backs
when I see Stanford

coming out of my cell
I pause and he sees me
seeing him

He unlocks my door
and waits for me
to get in

There, on my desk
is more paper
and a small watercolor set

like the ones
they give to kids

He nods without
looking at me and
closes the door

HOPE V

Kadon is the first one to start sitting with me

Then Smoke and Rah started coming, too
I'm not a teacher, but they watch me mix colors

and turn shapes into people, spaces, and ideas
And I ask them
Y'all ever heard of the butterfly effect?

They keep cracking jokes
and talking shit
Clowning me about
my little paint set

And I remember myself
before the dream
before the colors and shapes
before the old paintings
        by white artists
before the art history

when it was just me
in our apartment
on the floor

while the TV was on
Umi in the kitchen
making lamb and rice

Construction paper everywhere
Broken crayons everywhere
Coloring books everywhere

And me, small enough to fit
in the space between
the couch and coffee table

I colored outside the lines
I colored outside the boxes
                like freedom

So I take a sheet
of white construction paper
and the watercolor set
and make me a box
make me some blurred lines

curved and smudged
smooth and rounded
and make me a butterfly

This week
the district attorney
the prosecutor
and my new attorney, Tarana
will meet with Jeremy Mathis
who will be giving a statement

and as I tell the Corners
about how a butterfly can change
a big thing out there in the world

butterflies are fluttering in my belly

Delicate wings flapping
so fast
I can't even breathe right

I cover the page in butterflies
wondering if these butterflies
inside of me
will be the ones to
change the world

or maybe

Jeremy Mathis's
truth is the real butterflies

Whatever his words will be
they will come fluttering out of him

small things
that will change
one big thing in the world

      My life
      My whole damn life—

I spread my paintings out across all the tables

and the Corners make sure that no one
messes with them   Four small paintings

Watercolor on paper

Like Picasso's *Guernica*—butterflies with distorted wings
at war   at war   at war

like Dalí's *Persistence of Memory*—a watch
with pretty little wings trapped in its box

like da Vinci's *Mona Lisa*—a black mother
sitting still   hands on her lap   with no mouth

I remix all these famous paintings
with the supplies that I have

and put them into a yellow envelope
from Ms. Buford's office

I address it to Imani Dawson
and I write her a note

        This is what I want the world
            to know about me
                My art—

            My truth

A NOTE FROM THE AUTHORS

Yusef Salaam was fifteen years old when he followed a few of his friends into Central Park on a warm April evening in 1989. He'd been doing what he'd always done as a teen growing up in New York City. We both remember what us kids used to call just hanging out and fooling around: "Wilin' out." It's not a phrase that's meant to be written. So it's easy to misconstrue. It was easy for the media to misinterpret what was part of our vernacular as "Wilding," and turn it into something sinister in association with the infamous "Central Park jogger" case.

When Yusef first started writing, it was because, like many young brothers, he wanted to be a hip-hop artist. He'd been writing rhymes since he was eleven or twelve years old. The "Central Park Five" case, as it was known, happened during an era in music when message-driven hip-hop songs were popular. *Self Destruction*, KRS-One's *Love's Gonna Get'cha*, and especially Public Enemy were some of the artists and songs that shaped both of us as budding writers and were essentially the soundtrack to our young lives. We gravitated toward Public Enemy, who came out with a flow that sounded less like rap, and more like a truth-telling speech.

So when Yusef and four other teen boys were tried and convicted of a crime they did not commit, he and so many other young people, including myself, were awakened to the injustices of their country and of the world.

The "Central Park jogger" case was my earliest memory of bearing witness to injustice. All throughout my high school and college years, there were more violent acts committed against Black men and boys, including Yusuf Hawkins, who at sixteen was fatally shot in a predominantly white neighborhood in Brooklyn; Michael Griffith, who was chased out of a white neighborhood by a group of white teens and as a result, was fatally hit by a car; and the unarmed West African immigrant Amadou Diallo, who was shot forty-one times by cops just as he was entering his apartment in the Bronx. All these stories were why I wanted to become a journalist. I was so angry with the world that I had to find a way to speak truth to power.

So when Yusef and I met at Hunter College in 1999, just two years after he'd been released from prison and had not yet been exonerated, and ten years after the fateful night that changed his life forever, I wanted to be one of the few college reporters to investigate the truth about the "Central Park jogger" case, because so many of us believed those five teens were innocent. By sharing this story, I had hoped to expose the ongoing disparities in the criminal justice system and how the media continually portrays an imbalanced view of Black children.

When Yusef was convicted, it was the start of him realizing that he needed to speak his truth. He realized that this art form he'd been honing since childhood, hip-hop, was going to allow him to get his message across at this most critical point in his life.

While waiting for his sentence, Yusef was told that he should throw himself at the mercy of the court; that he should plead for the least amount of time possible. But he had been reading about Malcolm X and others who were in the struggle. He had been inspired by hip-hop artists who were using their platforms to spread powerful messages about our experiences, and he started writing instead. So when his sentence was handed down and Yusef was given the stage to speak his truth, he read a poem entitled, "I Stand Accused."

While *Punching the Air* is not Yusef's story, Amal's character is inspired by him as an artist and as an incarcerated teen who had the support of his family, read lots of books, and made art to keep his mind free. This book is infused with some of the poetry Yusef wrote while he was incarcerated. When we started to discuss what kind of story we wanted to tell, we started with a name—Amal, which means "hope" in Arabic. It was important that whatever this teen boy was going through, he should always have hope and we should write a story that instills hope for the reader. Yusef and I wanted people to know that when you find yourself in dark places, there's always a light somewhere in that darkness, and even if that light is inside of you, you can illuminate your own darkness by shedding that light on the world.

After meeting Yusef in college, we were reunited while I was touring for my debut novel, *American Street*. Yusef expressed his interest in speaking to more teens because his tragedy happened to him as a teen boy. He'd been mostly addressing law students and social justice and community organizations. A few days later, I approached him with the idea of telling his story in the form of a young adult book. We knew that young people needed to hear this story.

At the center of Amal's story is the cycle of racial violence that continues to plague this country. But this is not just a story about a crime or race. *Punching the Air* is about the power of art, faith, and transcendence in the most debilitating circumstances. It's our hope that all readers will experience the journey of a boy who finds himself in a heated moment where one wrong move threatens his future, and how he uses his art to express his truth, the truth.

—Ibi Zoboi and Yusef Salaam

ACKNOWLEDGMENTS

I am still amazed by how this book came together. I never set out to write about and from the perspective of an incarcerated teen. However, everything in the universe seemed to have made this such a smooth and serendipitous journey, and there are so many people to thank. First, I am beyond grateful to Yusef Salaam who has become like a brother and who trusted me from day one—from our chance meeting at Hunter College to our many conversations about how to share our truth with the world. It has been a tremendous honor to work with you on this book. You are one of the most compassionate, gracious, and insightful people I know. I am so grateful to our professor, Dr. Marimba Ani, who invited Yusef to join her class that day. The most magical moment when Yusef and I reunited was realizing that we both retained much of what we learned from Mama Marimba. This was a testament that we truly share a similar worldview. Shout-out to my Hunter crew, Daughters of Afrika, who are still my closest and dearest friends. My husband, Joseph, artist extraordinaire, another inspiration for this book. Thank you for your unwavering support and love.

Alessandra Balzer, my editor and my friend, who truly cares on such a deep level—this book would not be this book without your keen insight and attention to detail.

Thank you for valuing and respecting my vision and always offering a listening ear and encouraging words. You've gone above and beyond for this book and I appreciate you.

Thank you, Ammi-Joan Paquette, for believing in this project and being an early champion. Thank you to the team at Balzer + Bray and HarperCollins. Ebony LaDelle, there aren't enough words to express how grateful I am that you are in the room and seated at the table. You already know. A very special thanks to my agent, Tina Dubois. I'm so honored to have you as my champion and friend. Thank you to Jackie Burke in publicity and Jenna Stempel-Lobell and Alison Donalty for the design. To artists Temi Coker and Alexis Franklin for their incredible work on the cover, and Omar Pasha for the interior pieces.

Beyond grateful to our first readers, attorney Kenneth Montgomery, and award-winning playwright and prison reform activist Liza Jessie Peterson. Thank you for the work you do with our young people and for providing essential feedback for this book.

A huge heartfelt thanks to Jacqueline Woodson, Jason Reynolds, and Ibram X. Kendi. Your love for us is palpable, and I am because we are.

This book, all my books, my heart, and my love goes out to Black children all over the world whose genius is often stifled, muted, and blotted out before it can ever reach the stars. And to Black boys—my first crushes, my first dates, my homies, my little brothers, my son, my students—I prayed and continue to pray for your safety and I wish for your joy, your bliss. My freedom is your freedom is my freedom. We are links on a chain, bound to each other.

To the ancestors of the Middle Passage, whose shoulders we all stand on—each time we honor you, we stand a little bit taller.

—Ibi Zoboi

I don't believe in coincidences. The blessing of being able to run into someone from my past who knew me as a fearful, shy young man to the person that I am now, lets me know that everything happens on purpose and for a purpose. This collaboration was in the works before Ibi and I realized it was something we were going to do. We have a shared connection in Dr. Marimba Ani's class, where it was my introduction to African consciousness. It was a necessary addition to my experience, and then fast-forward to the present, someone from that class is a published author, and with her skills and talents, is able to help me tell my truth. I am so grateful for Ibi and thank you, God, for allowing our paths to cross in such a beautiful way.

To my umi, Sharonne Salaam, thank you for standing by me and raising me up in a world where there is a disdain for blackness and for providing me with the wherewithal to understand my place in it; for your tireless tenacity in boldly making sure the world never forgot "Yusef is Innocent"; and for being my rock and compass in times of darkness and light. Words cannot describe the depths of my love for you. We are taught that paradise lies at the feet of our mothers and I am thankful to have a mother that loves me and cares for me the way that you do.

A very special thanks and appreciation goes out to my

wife, Sanovia, and our blended family (in order): Nahtique, Dimani, Rain, Winter, Aaliyah, Poetry, Onaya, Ameerah, Assata, and baby Yusef Amir. Thank you for being patient with me and for being my sounding board to this work. To my sister, Aisha, for listening to much of my early work and encouraging me to continue on, and to my brother, Shareef, for his constant guidance and encouragement to dream bigger and plan better.

To the sacred brotherhood that became known as the Exonerated Five—Korey, Raymond, Antron, Kevin—thank you for being my companions on our collective journey. Having someone who knows exactly what you've gone through makes the road a little bit smoother. Thank you to Ken Burns, Sarah Burns, and Dave McMahon, and the *Central Park Five* documentary for giving us our voices back. To Ava Duvernay for her vision with *When They See Us*, thank you for giving us a bullhorn and a global platform to be able to speak truth to power about the injustices we faced.

To my team Frank Harris and Travis Linton, thank you for providing amazing guidance and direction in my professional life, and my team at CAA for being in my corner every step of the way.

To Alessandra Balzer, Ebony LaDelle, Jacqueline Burke, and the team at HarperCollins, I am so grateful for this opportunity to tell my truth with Ibi, and thank you for believing in me and our story.

To Jacqueline Woodson, Jason Reynolds, and Ibram X.

Kendi, thank you for your generous support and the work that you do for us.

What we are doing is sacred work. This is about breaking generational curses and adding to the greater good in hearts and minds. Thank you to the ancestors for passing down to us the legacy of resilience and grace. I am grateful for eyes that can see, a mouth that can speak, ears that can hear, and a heart full of faith.

—Dr. Yusef Salaam